# NOW AND LATER

### CHARITY TAHMASEB

Collins Mark Books

# Copyright

NOW AND LATER
*Copyright © 2015 by Charity Tahmaseb*

*Published by Collins Mark Books*
*Cover copyright © 2020 by Collins Mark Books*
*Cover design by Collins Mark Books*
*Cover art copyright © grandfailure/Depositphotos*

ISBN-13: 978-0-9987938-2-5
ISBN-10: 0-9987938-2-5

# Contents

# PART I

# Now
### TALES OF THE HERE AND NOW

## The Trouble with Firsts

THE FIRST TIME I rode a rollercoaster, I ended up with vomit in my shoes. Ian Chang dared me to ride with my hands in the air. When I refused, he sat behind me, voice loud and taunting in my ear. I clutched the bar and worked to keep the bologna and cheese in my stomach.

Ten seconds after the ride had come to a complete stop and we were standing on the platform, Ian threw up all over my shoes. His vomit soaked all the way through to my socks. The rest of our seventh grade orchestra screamed and ran away.

Our director looked like she wanted to throw herself onto the rollercoaster tracks. "Oh, Mattie." She clutched her hands together and stared at my shoes as if I'd purposely made vomit spew from them.

"Don't worry," Ian said. "I got this."

With each step down the stairs, my shoes made a horrid squishy sound, and I left a trail of smelly vomit prints. Ian used the remaining few bucks of his cash to buy me a pair of flip-flops. We threw my shoes and socks in the garbage. For the rest of the day he hung out with me, since I still smelled like vomit and no one else would come near me. We rode the antique cars five times and used the last of my money to split a snow cone.

That day, he went from being the annoying boy who stole my violin rosin to something else—what, exactly, is hard to say. He's still annoying. He still takes my violin rosin. But ever since, we've shared a music stand in orchestra and a lab table in honors science.

This is why first period physics is such a rollercoaster ride. Monday morning, when Ian plops down at our lab table, I don't even get a hello. All I get is, "You haven't asked him yet, have you?"

"How would you know?" Two can play this game.

"He doesn't look like the happiest man alive," Ian says. "That's why."

He knows I want Marcus Prescott to ask me to prom. In a perfect world, Marcus would. Of course, in a perfect world, he would say more than two words to me.

My plan: ask Marcus out first.

In theory, this is brilliant. In practice? I'm back on that rollercoaster, only this time, I'm the one about to vomit. If the road to hell is paved with good intentions, then the path to prom is strewn with crepe paper streamers and petals from dying corsages.

The thought of Marcus forces blood to my cheeks. "I'm afraid he'll say no." I am deathly afraid.

"He's a guy. He'll say yes." Ian gives me a *duh* sort of look. "It's what we do. Here, I'll prove it." He turns to face our physics class and raises his hands like he's addressing a political rally. "Poll for the guys," he says. "If a girl asks you out, do you say yes?"

The room erupts in agreement. Guys laugh and I hear a few "Yes's" in response.

I shrink in my chair, hoping no one connects me with Ian's question.

"She does the paying, too," someone says. "Right?"

"Of course." Ian gives me a significant look. "*Told you so,*" he mouths, and plops back down.

The class settles. Then, from the back, "Yeah, unless she's a dog."

My face burns. I keep my eyes straight ahead, refusing to even glance at Ian. He's all bouncy arms and legs next to me, trying to get me to look at him. I won't. I can't. There are some things you don't want people to see. Right now, my expression is one of them.

Ian grabs my notebook. Across the top of the page, he scrawls: *You are NOT a dog!!!*

He underlines NOT three times, just so I get the point. But he's written it across my physics homework. That's due today. In five minutes.

Now I glare at him.

"But it's true," Ian says. "You're actually—" He stops.

I fight the urge to place a finger beneath his chin and close his mouth. Only one thing can cause a complete Ian system shutdown. I swivel in my seat in time to see Rebecca Rinaldi glide into the room. Sure, most girls walk, but not our Rebecca. She floats, head perfectly tilted as if the prom queen tiara already perches there. She is high school royalty to Ian's court jester.

Here's something else about me and Ian: When it comes to crushes, our reach exceeds our grasp.

"You haven't asked her yet, have you?" Sure, I'm being smug, but I know it's true. Ever since Rebecca broke up with Colin Matterson, half the male population of Fremont High has been scheming to ask her to prom. Not that any of them have the nerve.

This especially includes Ian.

"It's all about timing." He waves a hand in the air. "And the right gesture."

"What if someone gestures first?"

Ian looks at me like I've said something obscene. "Colin put out the word that anyone who does has a death wish." He sits back and crosses his arms over his chest, stealing some of my smugness. "Thins out the competition."

"So. *You* have a death wish," I say. "I'll keep that in mind for our final project."

Ian laughs. "Come on, if I ask her, Colin will think it's a joke." He grins at me, all charm and laughing eyes. I can tell this is part of his plan. "Who takes me seriously?"

No one. But even as I think this, his face has never looked so solemn.

———

THE FIRST TIME I saw Marcus Prescott, my velvet orchestra skirt was pooled around my feet. It was the ninth grade band and orchestra fall concert. I stood with the other strings while the band streamed past, all shiny horns and gleaming woodwinds. I saw this amazing looking saxophone, carried by this amazing-looking boy with blond hair that dipped into his eyes, so I spun. Something snagged. Then, *pop!*

My thighs got cold, my feet extra warm. Unlike seventh grade, no one could run away. The boys snickered and the girls gasped. But Ian was there, grabbing for his violin case, letting it thunk to the floor. While everyone went, "Shhhh!" he opened the case to reveal my violin rosin and several safety pins. He pinned me so my skirt bunched up in the back. Then, as if to make it all better, he lifted his cummerbund. There was his own wardrobe malfunction. Keeping his pants up was a series of interlocking safety pins. He looked so proud.

Even today, I don't know if Marcus ever got a peek at my pantyhose. But music is the reason I'm standing between the orchestra and band rooms on Tuesday morning. Well, music and Marcus. He likes to grab one of the practice rooms before first bell—something I know with stalker-like precision.

I'm clutching my violin case to my chest like it's my shield. When footfalls echo down the hall, my fingers grow slick. Marcus comes into view, and the case nearly slips from my grasp. My heart pounds. I'm convinced Marcus can hear it. He slows down. Then he stops. In front of me. He smiles.

"Hey, Mattie."

Music, Marcus and Mattie. How perfect does that sound? We're made for each other. I know it. It's this knowledge that pushes me through everything—the fear gripping my throat, my terrible luck with first times, the unbelievable way he's looking at me. All of it.

"Hey." The word comes out shaky, but he doesn't seem to notice. "I hear you like movies." And by "hear," I mean Ian asked for me without letting Marcus know he was asking for me.

Marcus nods.

"The Campus Film Society is doing their spring film festival." I shrug, going for casual. "They're playing some good ones on Thursday."

Last night, my best friend Claire and I decided Thursday was the best first-date night. No competition with Friday night plans or Saturday parties, but close enough to the weekend to count as a real date.

I hold my breath, but Marcus doesn't say anything. All that happens is a slight smile tugs at one corner of his mouth, like he's waiting for something—or waiting for me.

"Would you like to go?" My words sound almost breezy, considering the vice grip on my stomach. I'm surprised I haven't hurled all over his shoes. "With me?"

For a moment, he merely stares. Then I find my answer in the smile that tugs at both corners of his mouth.

————

THE FIRST TIME I ever drove our car, I backed into our mailbox. There's still a dent, above the left fender, that Dad never bothered having fixed.

"It's part of the legacy," he says whenever Mom brings it up.

Now I wonder if Marcus will notice the dent. Of

8

course, he might never see it. My hands shake so hard, I can barely make the turn for his driveway. Then, when he's all buckled in, I can't seem to find reverse.

"Relax," he says.

My cheeks flame. I'm certain I'll throw up, right here. In the car. On Marcus. It's only when I pull into a parking lot on campus that the tension leaves my shoulders and my stomach settles. Fremont State College is like a second home. Dad teaches physics here. I grew up riding my bike around the mall fountain and playing hide and seek in the department lounge.

When both the cashier in the Student Union and the guy taking tickets call me by name, Marcus looks just the tiniest bit impressed. All my misgivings melt away. This really *is* the perfect first date.

"You pick the movie," I tell Marcus. Our choices are limited to an action flick with an aging, Hollywood bald-guy type, a documentary, and a 1950s musical.

My heart sinks, just a little, when he chooses the action movie. I thought for sure he'd pick the musical. We share a bag of popcorn and our fingers meet as we both search for our next handful. It takes me at least thirty seconds to recover each time this happens, and I lose all sense of the plot. His choice doesn't seem so bad after all.

He doesn't put his arm around me, but he sits close. His body warms mine. He's a mix of sweat and spice, like warm gingersnaps. I decide this is the way a boy should smell.

On our way out, we fall in with a group of college students who think we're freshmen here on campus. The topic turns to majors (of course), and thanks to both Dad and honors physics, I can fake-talk my way through freshmen level courses.

"Who's your advisor?" one guy asks. He's cute in a scruffy kind of way. "I got Collins. Man, what a dick."

Okay. Now? He's just scruffy. "I haven't really declared yet," I say. "But I know who you're talking about."

Sure, I know Professor Collins. I know him so well, I'll be seeing him when I get home. Marcus looks like he's about to burst. He grabs my hand and we run toward my car. He's laughing when we get there.

"Classic," he says over the roof of the car. "You should've told him who your dad is. I would've loved to have seen his face then."

I think we fly all the way to Marcus's house. But in the driveway, I have a three-second heart attack. Do I get out and walk him to the door? Lean in for a hug? A kiss? But Marcus flings open the car door and bounds up the porch steps before I can even kill the ignition.

He waves, then vanishes inside. Thus, our official first date ends. I survived. I think. Maybe my trouble with firsts is all in the past.

———

ON THE FIRST DAY of Kindergarten, I left my lunch on the floor of the car. Someone stole all my glue sticks, and the teacher kept calling me Matilda instead of Mattie. Boys from my class chanted, "Matilda, Matilda" on the playground until the older kids took up the cry. By the end of the day, the whole school knew my name.

When my mom picked me up, she was pleased I'd

made so many new friends. I couldn't tell her that not only was I the girl with no real friends, but I had zero glue sticks to show for it.

The next day, my "cubby buddy" passed me one of her glue sticks, the purple kind with glitter. We've been best friends ever since, and Claire has never once called me Matilda.

So of course, it's Claire who's sitting beside me when on Friday, Marcus swings by our table at lunch. "Hey, man!" he calls out, the perfect imitation of a frat-boy wannabe. "What's your major?" Then? He winks and keeps going to his regular table.

Claire clutches my arm. All the other girls around us have that gaping mouth, wide-eyed fish look.

"Deets!" is the only thing Claire can get out.

"Not much to tell," I say, but no one believes me. I rehash the date. In this version, I'm not nearly as nervous and much wittier when talking to the college guys. It's possible Marcus remembers it this way, too. I even make his flying leap from the car sound funny not frantic.

"Prom." Claire breathes the word. "We can double."

I shake my head. "Never came up," I say. Despite everything, prom feels as far away as ever.

"But he's into you," she says. "Maybe you should ask him out again."

"What?"

"He might think he blew it or something. That's why he ran from the car."

The heat in my cheeks goes up a notch.

"But if you ask him out again—" Claire places a hand

on mine, locking me in place, insisting on my full attention— "then he knows he didn't blow it. Get it?"

I nod automatically, convinced I can't do this a second time, even as my mind churns out ideas. I hit upon one. Just like that, all my doubts vanish.

———

THE FIRST TIME I took our dog Einstein for a walk, he looped the leash around my ankles so many times I toppled like a felled tree. Today I pass the leash from hand to hand while Einstein gallops back and forth, completely wound up by the Fremont High boys track team streaming by.

A dog, I think, is an even better prop than a violin. Already a few guys from the team have paused in their trek, jogging in place while Einstein sniffs their shoes. He's a big, sloppy mutt (Einstein the dog, not Einstein the physicist). Even Claire, who's allergic to dogs, loves him.

In the distance, I catch sight of Ian's impossibly long legs tearing up the path. A few whispered words to him during Honors English 12, and my idea became a plan. Now it looks like he's sprinting to make that plan work.

His breath is ragged when he reaches me. He swipes his bangs from his eyes and his sweat dots my face. "Sorry," he pants.

I pass the leash from one hand to the other to keep Einstein from tripping me. He loves Ian and would follow him home if I let him.

"You've got a window. He's right behind me." Ian

glances over my shoulder. "There isn't anyone for another minute. He's all yours."

"You're the best," I call as he starts down the path.

Ian spins, holds his arms out wide. "Tell me something I don't know." He sprints off without another word.

In a second, I see the glint of blond hair, darkened by sweat. The approaching boy looks hot—and I mean that in so many ways. He wears black compression shorts beneath the ultra-short track variety and a matching tank.

"Hey!" Marcus shouts. "Have you seen Ian? Intervals, my ass. He's sprinting."

"He's…" I wave a hand in the air, indicating Ian was both here and gone.

Marcus slows to a jog. "Nice dog."

Einstein settles at my feet, sitting upright, like he's on guard.

"He must be tired from everyone running past," I say, "he's normally not this calm."

Marcus nods. I think he's about to swing onto the path again, and my heart leaps in my chest, starts beating as if I'm the one who's been sprinting.

Instead, he says, "Any more of those movies playing?"

I know this is a gift. Maybe it's karma, making up for all those terrible firsts. But what really matters is I have an opening. "Sunday night is the festival finale." I pause, for a heartbeat, for a breath, for the time it takes a butterfly to flap her wings.

Marcus drops his gaze, to his shoes, then Einstein. He looks at the playground behind us, then toward the path where Ian vanished. "What?" He seems almost startled by his own voice. "Yeah. Sure. Why not." He glances at the path again. "I gotta go catch that bastard." He takes off down the path. He's thirty feet away when he stops dead. "Tell you what," he calls. "My treat this time, and I'll drive."

He flies down the path, taking my heart with him.

———

THE FIRST TIME I ever used Mom's credit card, my hand shook so badly I tore the receipt. They insisted on seeing my ID and then, called my parents anyway. Today I can feel it burn a hole in my purse, but that's not why my hands are shaking.

"You've got to get it," Claire says.

I'm standing in the prom dress section of Macy's department store, an incredible silk, lace, and tulle version of me staring back in triplicate. "It's jinxing it, don't you think?"

"You guys are going out tomorrow night, right?"

I nod.

"And he's driving and paying? Right?"

Again, I nod.

"And I bet after that," Claire says, her voice triumphant, "he's going to ask you to prom."

But he hasn't. It's this one tiny fact that keeps me in the dress and indecisive. Once I pull out Mom's credit card, there's no going back. I'm committed to prom, whether Marcus asks me or I take Einstein.

"This dress won't be here on Monday." Claire's right. Girls started shopping for prom weeks ago; I'm lucky to find something this good, in my size, still on the rack.

"Technically," I say, my voice as tentative as my words. "I don't have a date to prom."

"And that's just a technicality." Claire grips me by the shoulders. "Second date. He's paying." She gives me a little shake. "He's into you and probably just wants to ask you somewhere nice, not when he's all sweaty from track practice."

What Claire says makes perfect sense—perfect dream-come-true sense. But doubt still eats away at my insides. First prom, first formal dress. My gaze scans the dress department as if one of the mannequins will come to life and pronounce some sort of guiding prophecy.

They don't, of course. All I have to guide me is that second date with Marcus and Claire's unrelenting scowl.

Second date. No more trouble with firsts.

I pull out Mom's credit card, and Claire's frown melts into a grin.

―――――

THE FIRST TIME MARCUS PRESCOTT picks me up, he taps the horn lightly as he pulls into our driveway. Einstein barks. I jump, grab my purse.

Dad glances from the stack of papers he's grading. "He's not coming in?"

The parent meet-and-greet? Talk about a jinx. I slide open my phone and check the time. "We're late."

"No." Dad writes an F and *See me* on the paper he's grading. "*He's* late."

I dash out, pretending I don't hear.

On campus, we get popcorn to share. Tradition, I

think. We have a tradition! The salt sucks all the moisture from my mouth—or maybe that's excitement. I barely watch the film Marcus lets me pick. My heart pounds; my cheeks feel flushed. I'm still like this when the movie ends and we're walking across campus. The way to the parking lot is lit with so many streetlamps, it's like some strange, golden day.

"So," Marcus says. "Did you like that?"

I want to say, *Only because of you.* But that's territory for a third date or even prom. So I just nod.

He holds open the car door for me. As I get in, he says, "You know, it's been really good getting to know you."

The door slams, and I hear his unspoken word. *But...*

I ignore the warning. When he slips into the driver's side seat, I blurt, "Will you go to prom with me?"

Marcus stares straight ahead, his hands clutching the steering wheel. When he finally turns toward me, I know he's going to tell me something I don't want to hear. My heart feels like it's pumping ice crystals. My mind scans the last several days. I hear the echo of Claire's words. *He's into you.*

But he's not. It's clear in the way he looks at me, at the way he plucks the steering wheel. I'm not the girl he wants in his car.

"Here's the thing," he says. "I really admire you, but—"

I bite my lower lip.

"There's this girl. I mean, I couldn't even ask her out."

Clearly, this girl isn't me. The taste of copper floods my mouth.

Marcus continues as if he hasn't noticed I'm mauling my lower lip. "Not until you...well, inspired me."

So this is *my* fault? I'm gagging. "Who?" I ask. He owes me that.

His fingers stumble in their trek across the steering wheel. Even in the yellow lamplight he looks bright red. "Rebecca Rinaldi?" He says it like it's a question.

Oh.

So.

Predictable.

I can't say a word, and he puts the car in gear and pulls from the lot. The second the wheels hit the asphalt, I realize why he wanted to drive. My hands are shaking so hard, I can barely hold my purse. Everything blurs. I don't remember the way home.

And for three whole seconds, I believe that driving us both off a cliff is a very, very good idea.

I'm surprised when Marcus pulls into the driveway and turns off the ignition. One, I don't remember my own driveway. Two, I'm kind of shocked he doesn't slow down, open the door, and make me tuck and roll.

"Hey," he says when my hand reaches for the door handle. "We can still be friends. I mean that."

Sure he does.

Then he reaches over and pats my knee. My *knee*. The traitorous thing tingles at his touch. Then it burns. I think I might shatter. I step out of the car carefully, like I'm navigating rocky terrain. One false step, and I'll plummet.

Inside, I lean against the thick oak of the front door. My mind latches onto the word *friend*. But it's not Marcus I think of.

It's Ian.

My stomach clenches. The tears flirting at the corners of my eyes dry up. I propel myself upstairs and boot up my laptop. Before I can send an email, Ian pings me on IM.

**Ian: Home too soon.**

I decide on quick and to the point.

**Mattie: Have you asked R yet?**

**Ian: Moment's not right. You?**

**Mattie: Someone else is going to ask her.**

**Ian: Proof.**

**Mattie: It's Marcus.**

For several seconds, the cursor blinks at me. Ian's icon isn't grayed out, but the virtual silence feels wrong. At last, a message appears.

**Ian: W...T...F happened tonite?**

**Mattie: Nothing.**

**Ian: BS**

**Mattie: Drop it, ok.**

**Ian: Can I do s/t?**

**Mattie: Yeah. Ask R to prom.**

I log off. A minute later, my phone buzzes. I hit ignore. When Ian pings me with text messages, I shut it down too and crawl into bed. In the dark, I can see the outline of my closet and the monster inside it—in the form of a cream and gold prom dress.

I don't remember crying, but in the morning my pillow is damp.

———

THE FIRST TIME I played in a string quartet, Ian poked me in the eye with his bow. Tears blazed a path of mascara down my cheek, but I didn't miss a note.

Today, in the cafeteria, I swear I hear the sound of strings, but my heart hurts so much the rest of my body refuses to move. I think my bones will calcify like this. I'll become some permanent and pathetic cafeteria fixture. Years from now, seniors will lead freshmen girls past, whispering, "This is what happens when you ask a guy out."

A hum in the air pulls me from my stupor. Violin. Viola. After a scrape of a chair, a cello joins in. Dead center of the cafeteria, four members of the Fremont High orchestra play. On first violin? Ian. Their audience? The varsity cheerleader table—or, more accurately, Rebecca Rinaldi at the varsity cheerleader table.

I want to reach out and make sure Ian doesn't miss a note. I want the music to soar. I want Ian to win.

Something twists inside me. For the briefest second, I don't want Rebecca to say yes.

But she's sitting there, hands clasped, looking like she's about to squeal. When Ian trades his violin for a single cream-colored rose, the entire cafeteria goes nuts—cheering, table pounding, foot-stomping crazy.

Rebecca throws her arms around Ian, and I content myself with this:

He's won.

————

THE FIRST TIME I talk to my prom date, it's through Facebook chat.

Claire's cousin, Jason Abernathy, is some sort of superstar baseball player over at Olympia High School. In the yearbook poll, he was voted most popular and life of the party. His nickname is The Ab.

Honestly, this last tidbit is so disturbing that I almost don't respond to the friend request. Then I remember the monster inside my closet and click through to Jason's profile.

Within seconds, a chat box pops up.

**Jason: Yo! So we're on for prom?**

*Why, yes*, I think, *it's nice to meet you too.*

**Mattie: I guess. You ok with it?**

Jason: At first, I thought Matilda = dog but C showed me your pic. Chzzzzz.

Chzzzz? I look like cheese, not a dog?

Jason: That's the sound of water hitting something hot. Cuz you know, you're hot and all.

Good looks *and* he's poetic. I really hit the jackpot.

Mattie: At least I don't look like cheese.

Jason: Huh?

Mattie: Never mind. Hey, want to go out before prom? Get to know each other?

I'm praying he'll say yes. Prom as a first date? If recent history is any indication, I haven't lost my trouble with firsts.

Jason: No can do, babe. Booked solid with proms thru end of the month.

So. I'm going to prom with a Rent-a-Hottie.

Jason: I can call you babe since we're going to prom, right?

Mattie: Just don't call me cheese.

THE FIRST THING JASON says to me when he slips the silk flowers onto my wrist is, "I'll need this back."

I hold my hand away from me and wonder how many wrists have worn this particular corsage. I glance up a Jason, gauging whether he's serious. The big, goofy grin makes him look innocent.

I know better.

"I have two more proms and a cotillion," he adds.

So much for scrapbooking this. "Sure," I say. Because really? I could take the flowers off right now. They're lilac, my gown a shimmering gold. I look like an overdressed Vikings fan.

Jason's a hit even before the grand march starts. He's all high fives and fist bumps. It's possible he knows more people at my school than I do. We snake our way through the line for the grand march, weaving around and then into the college ballroom.

I purposely don't glance around. Rumor has it Marcus asked someone else to prom. That's not something I need to see.

Then Jason's voice booms beside me. "Yo, Marco!"

"Marcus." The correction is automatic, and I hear the strain in Marcus's voice. This is the last place he wants to be, too.

"Hey, you do that music thing," Jason says. "You must know Mattie." He yanks me around so I have no choice but to confront Marcus. Jason nods, like what he's about to say is common knowledge. "She's hot. Chzzzz."

Normally, I might cringe at this. Instead I'm fixated.

Not on Marcus so much as his date. I don't know her. I don't *want* to know her. But she must know about me since she won't look me in the eye. Neither will Marcus. I've never been kicked in the stomach, but I imagine it feels just like this. No breath, no words. Pain radiates over me.

Somehow I keep walking. I nod when Jason says things. Vaguely, I hope I'm not agreeing to anything illegal. We inch forward, waiting to cross the "bridge of dreams" and officially arrive at prom. When footsteps sound on the ramp above, I glance up.

Rebecca Rinaldi floats by in a dress that resembles a delicate pink cloud and looks about as substantial. Ian wears his black orchestra tux. Our eyes meet. It's me and him in this ballroom, alone—no people, no music. For a second, I know what it's like to have his arm linked with mine.

Once we cross the bridge, Jason vanishes. I mean that literally. After fifteen minutes, I realize his offer to get drinks is a ruse. Maybe he double-booked proms and is racing back and forth between the two. The idea is funny and keeps me—almost—oblivious to the couples around me until Marcus blocks my view of the dance floor.

"Hey." He stares at his shoes, then raises his head, halfway, to peer at me. It's a killer move. If he'd used it on Rebecca Rinaldi, she would've gone to prom with him. He holds out a hand. "Want to dance?"

I let him lead me onto the dance floor. Someone turns the glitter ball up to max sparkle. It's like dancing among the stars. I don't know the song, but I pick out the strings

—the violin, the viola—right away. It makes me think of Ian.

In that moment, I wish upon one of those fake stars. I really do hope he's having a good time, the best time. Just as I send my wish skyward, Marcus pulls me close, the kind of close that should only happen with a real prom date.

I step away.

"Mattie, what... I mean..."

I feel oddly alone, even with all these people around me, even with Marcus a whisper away. He holds out his hand, but this time I don't take it. Instead, I lift the skirt of my dress off the floor and walk away from the ballroom.

———

OUTSIDE, the air cools my bare shoulders. I sit on the wall that surrounds the parking lot. It's just high enough that I can kick my feet, except I'm not in the mood for that. I study the real stars above me and catch the hint of a song when the ballroom doors open and close.

I hear the footsteps long before I can see anyone. My heartbeat keeps time with their cadence until the footfalls stutter. Now the sound is more like clomping. Only when both Jason and Marcus land in front of me do I see why: they're in the middle of a shoving match. They both drop their arms when they see my glare.

"Someone told me you left," Jason says. "You're not pissed or anything, are you?"

"Someone?" I ask. "Or Claire?"

Jason actually blushes.

"Mattie, I just want to say—"

I hold up a hand, stopping Marcus.

It hits me then. I don't want to be at prom with either boy. Marcus isn't who I thought he was. Or maybe, my idea of Marcus never matched who he really is. Part of me still goes a little melty at the thought of him. But mostly? I'm not sure I even like him.

Maybe it's the fake bridge, and the fake stars, but adding a fake date? Nothing is lonelier than that. I'd rather be at prom by myself.

"Thanks for being my Rent-a-Hottie," I tell Jason. "But you don't have to stay."

"You sure?" He looks perplexed. "I don't mind. You're pretty hot in that dress." He licks his finger then presses it to his butt. "Chzzzz."

"Oh, I'm sure."

"Then do you mind?" He waves toward the parking lot. "There's this other girl—"

"You're double booked?" I feign hurt surprise.

"Claire said she'd kill me if I ditched you, but since..." he trails off.

"Go." I almost say *have fun*, but I'm not sure if what he's doing qualifies as fun.

He moves to weave his way through the parked cars, phone pressed to his ear, when he spins around. He points toward my wrist. I peel off the corsage and hold it out, its strap between my index finger and thumb. Jason snatches it and dashes off, ready to be someone else's dream date.

Then it's just me and Marcus and the prom that isn't and never was.

I push off from the wall and shake out my skirt.

"Hey, Mattie." His voice is gentle. "You don't suppose we could try this again?"

If he had said those words a week ago, I would've melted into Mattie goo. But now? I want to point out he brought someone else to prom. If he can't see how wrong that is, then there's nothing I can do about it.

"No." I lift the hem of my skirt. "I don't suppose we can."

———

I'M THREADING through the maze of cars and limos when someone calls my name. I turn to see Ian's truck, tailgate down, with him sitting on the bed, legs stretched out and crossed at the ankle.

"You okay?" he asks.

"Fine, but why—"

"I saw Tweedledee and Tweedledum go after you. I figured you could handle it." He shrugs. "But just in case."

"Thanks," I say.

"It's what friends do."

Funny how the word sounds so different when Ian says it. I wonder where *his* date is. So I ask, because that's what friends do. "Where's Rebecca?"

"Probably still puking behind Colin's stretch Hummer. I think he's holding her hair." Ian shrugs again. "I told her the sushi smelled off." He looks totally unfazed.

"What happened?" I clutch my arms, willing the goose bumps away. "I mean, other than food poisoning."

"Partway through the first dance, she decided she was at prom with the wrong person."

"Oh, Ian." My heart feels tight and tender in my chest. "I'm so sorry."

"I'm not." He stares at me, hard. "During the grand march, about the time I was crossing the bridge, I realized *I* was at prom with the wrong person." Ian hops from the truck bed and drapes his tux jacket around my shoulders.

I inhale. Then, I melt. Completely. He smells like a boy —like a friend—should. "Ian, would you go to the last hour of prom with me?"

His fingers come to rest on my cheek. "I was hoping you'd ask."

The first time I kiss Ian Chang, I get a mouthful of his nose. As for second kisses?

Let's just say that's between friends.

*The Trouble with Firsts* was first published as part of *The First Time* e-anthology, October 2011, edited by Rhonda Stapleton and Jessica Verday.

## Glass Slipper

THE TRUCK RUMBLED down the hill, the engine loud enough to wake the sun. I resented the fact it woke me so early every Saturday morning, with its tires crunching up gravel like breakfast cereal. The thing looked like it had driven straight out of *The Grapes of Wrath* and onto the gravel road behind our house, its paint the same dusty color as the road except for one egg-shell-blue fender.

I resented the fact that the egg-shell blue fender was the exact color of the prom dress hanging in my closet. I resented the fact that the man driving the truck was the great uncle of the boy who was no longer taking me to prom.

Once upon a time, that boy and I were best friends. Once upon a time, we did everything together. Somehow, along the way, we'd lost that once upon a time. But today? Today, I was getting it back.

I slipped from bed, not bothering to do more than shove feet into sneakers and yank my hair into a ponytail. Outside, the sky was a deep purple. The air bathed my burning cheeks and the skin on my arms puckered. I felt brave, but only because I hadn't taken a step off the front porch. If I didn't move soon, I'd stay rooted in place until the sun turned the sky the color of that one, blue fender.

I'd crept down the gravel road behind my house countless times. The soles of my feet anticipated the sharpness of certain rocks. My knees knew when the road curved and became almost too steep.

The one thing I wasn't expecting was a lone dress shoe in the center of the gravel road, halfway between the top of the hill and the old workshop at the bottom. I inched closer, the shoe's appearance too odd to be any kind of trap, but my body didn't believe it. Something about this had to be magical—a men's size eleven black dress shoe sitting in the middle of nowhere? It was like finding Cinderella's glass slipper, only in reverse.

I crouched, my gaze darting from side to side, as if someone were spying on me. Then, I reached out and grabbed the shoe. With it tucked in one hand, I continued down the hill and toward the workshop.

When we were little, Trey and I would sneak around his great uncle's workshop, with its weathered boards and cracked window glass. In the rain, the wood looked like chocolate, the windows like glazed sugar. We'd clutch hands and pretend to be Hansel and Gretel. We both knew there had to be a mystery inside. In March, when Trey started working for his great uncle, he told me:

"No mystery. Mostly junk."

By the time I reached the rear fender of the truck, that men's dress shoe was slick with sweat from my hand. From inside the workshop came hammering followed by a saw tearing through wood, the vibration of both rattling my jaw. Were there any answers inside? Or mostly junk?

I pretended not to see the egg-shell blue fender. But the sky had lightened, and the windshield captured the color in its reflection. If you wanted to, you could imagine an egg-shell blue ribbon leading you all the way up to the sky, or to prom, or at least somewhere that didn't reek of oil, and rotting timber, and dust.

I tiptoed across nails and dodged planks. Uncle Dmitri always locked the front door but never the back.

"It's how I sneak in when I'm late," Trey told me once.

With the shoe trapped under my arm, I pressed one hand against the door while the other turned the rusty knob. With each burst of noise from a hammer or saw, I pushed the door open another inch, all the while wondering if this was worth it. Was Trey worth it?

All the kids in the neighborhood called Trey's uncle "Crazy old Dmitri." My mom always said he was just a man who'd lived a hard life and wanted to be alone most of the time. Trey liked to pretend they weren't even related. Considering he started working for his uncle this spring, that was kind of hard to do.

As for me? I was beginning to think crazy ran in that family. Why else would Trey stand at our lunch table yesterday and announce—in front of a packed cafeteria— that he wasn't taking me to prom?

The only other thing he said was: "I'm sorry."

Then he ran from the cafeteria. The murmurs that flowed in his wake sounded like water rushing over rocks.

So yesterday at 11:58 a.m., I had a prom date. At 12:01 p.m., I did not. Prom was today. Our families still thought we were going. My prom dress still hung in the closet. And now, I was stalking my former best friend and some lonely old man—while still in my pajamas.

Maybe I was the one who was crazy.

Inside the workshop, sun streamed through high windows, the rays catching sawdust that floated in the air, making the space look almost magical. Almost. I stepped over stacked lumber and ducked under cobwebs, their thin strands brushing my face and arms. I wasn't afraid of spiders or dirt or anything that might pop from a corner in this old workshop.

"Mira?"

At the voice, I jerked upright, and my head went straight through a thick web. My heart pounded loud enough to rival the hammering, which I now noticed had stopped. No, I wasn't afraid of anything in this old workshop, except for maybe the person standing behind me.

I turned, slowly. The shoe slipped from my hand and plopped into sawdust, the fresh smell of it filling my nose.

"What are you doing here?" Trey asked.

"I—" Really, what was I doing here? In my pajamas? After yesterday, I was certain nothing could be more humiliating than being dumped by your prom date in the middle of the cafeteria. Well, I was wrong. This topped that. Run away? Or complete the cycle of humiliation?

The choice was mine.

"Why ... won't you take me to prom?"

Won't? Or can't? Don't want to? Or unable to? In this case, semantics mattered.

Trey sighed and ran a hand through his hair. Bits of

sawdust fluttered to the ground like tiny wooden snowflakes. "The thing is, I don't have any tickets."

I blinked. "But you picked up your tux—"

"Yeah. Since I don't have a credit card I had to pre-pay for that, so I went along when all the guys got theirs."

"I'm still confused about the tickets."

"I thought I'd be able to scrape the money together in time, but—" He shook his head. "They sold out long before that happened."

Cold dread wormed its way inside me, leaving a trail of shame in its wake. Where had my head been these last few weeks? Up in a cloud of tulle and silk. The real me would've noticed something was wrong with Trey. So I asked the question I should have months ago.

"What's going on?"

"Let's see." Trey started counting items off on his fingers. "I have a tux minus one shoe—which I'm sure they'll charge me for—no prom tickets, enough money so we can eat at McDonald's, as long as we don't splurge, and my uncle just slipped me five bucks so I can buy you a corsage."

I peered through the darkness for Uncle Dmitri.

"He went outside," Trey added. "He's smart enough not to smoke in here."

"Oh."

"It's like he lives in 1970 or something. You don't want to know what I make an hour, but when he heard I was taking you to prom, he gave me a bonus." He paused, then added, "A whole dollar a week."

"Why didn't you—?"

He held up a hand, stopping my words. "I thought I

could pull it together, really take you to prom, you know, like Kyle and Lindsey—not the stretch Hummer or anything—but a real prom."

"I don't need a real prom." But I'd been acting like it—for months now. My gaze took in Trey, sweat-soaked and flecked with tiny pieces of wood. Tall and silent and trying to create something from nothing. I glanced down at the lone shoe hidden in the sawdust.

"We can still go to prom," I said, the spark of an idea spreading a grin across my face.

"We don't have tickets."

"Who needs tickets?"

"We can't crash prom."

"Why not?"

"Name me one person who's done it." Trey crossed his arms over his chest, like he knew I didn't have an answer.

I thought for a moment. "Cinderella." I bent down and fished the shoe from the drift of sawdust. "And look, I found your glass slipper."

"Doesn't Cinderella lose her shoe after the ball?"

"We're doing everything backwards."

———

AT 7:55 THAT EVENING, I took another walk down the gravel road behind my house. This time, the rocks felt jagged and treacherous against the thin soles of my ballet flats. I clutched handfuls of egg-shell blue silk taffeta, holding the skirt's hem well above the dirt.

Outside the workshop, Trey stood so still and so rigid, I thought maybe his uncle had taken up wood carving and had left this particular version of his nephew outside to ward off evil spirits. But wood carvings never flushed with the barest hint of pink. They never, to my knowledge, smiled.

Trey did both.

"You came," he said.

"Why wouldn't I?" But my stomach turned over on itself. I'd worried about the same thing, getting all dressed up with nowhere to go—or with anyone, for that matter.

Trey shrugged as if reading my thoughts. "You look great."

"You too."

Then, with the setting sun, awkwardness spread across the land. Prom couples everywhere were staring at each other, wondering what to do next.

"How are we going to get there?" Trey asked.

"We could walk." The prom was being held in the local college's ballroom. Sure, it was up a huge, steep hill, but Trey and I had walked it before.

"In those." He pointed.

I still clutched the dress high, so it was easy to see that while my ballet flats were dyed an egg-shell blue, they also had all the substance of actual egg shells.

This time, I shrugged. Once upon a time, we were supposed to tag along with Lindsey and Kyle, in that rented stretch Hummer, but they were already at dinner, miles away.

"Well, would you look at that!"

The voice made us both jump. Trey's eyes went wide, his face stricken. He mouthed something that might have been obscene.

"It's little Mira Swenson, only she's not so little anymore." With this comment, Uncle Dmitri nudged Trey in the ribs.

"It's nice to see you again, Mr. Leonov," I said. Despite the warm night, Trey's uncle wore a flannel shirt with his overalls. He was, in fact, the only person I'd ever seen who wore overalls the way they were designed to be worn—with hammers and rulers hanging from loops, pockets stuffed with nails and rags and who-knew-what.

"Trey," his uncle said, turning toward him, a frown clouding his expression. "Where's her corsage?"

Trey's gaze darted to mine, his eyes filled with the same panic I saw before pop quizzes. Where *was* my five-dollar corsage that he never bought?

"My fridge," I said. "My mom put it in there so it wouldn't wilt. We'll pick it up before we leave."

Trey mouthed, "Thank you."

Uncle Dmitri's brows drew together as if he expected us to leave, right then. Trey shifted from foot to foot. I realized I was still gripping the silk of my dress and tried to unclench my fingers.

"And how are you going to get there?" his uncle said, although it wasn't a question for either of us. He dug around in his overall pockets, at last drawing out a set of keys. Carefully, eyes downcast, he worried a single key from the ring and handed it to Trey.

"She's not fancy, but she'll get you there."

We were halfway up the hill, the old wheels spinning, the engine chugging, when I turned to Trey.

"Cinderella," I said.

"Huh?"

"You even have a fairy godmother."

———

"SO, HOW ARE WE GETTING IN?" Trey asked.

We stood at the ballroom's entrance, watching couple after couple parade inside.

"Well, I Googled it," I began.

Trey gave me a sidelong glance.

"Not much help," I added. "We were supposed to get here hours ago and pretend we were part of the maintenance crew."

He snorted.

Just then, Lindsey ran up to us. "You guys! You made it!" She cast me a worried look, one that said *is everything okay?*

I shrugged and mouthed, "No tickets."

Lindsey was the sort of girl no one ever questioned. Her round face radiated innocence, and all the teachers knew her from AP classes and honor roll. So when she dragged me in through one door, telling the chaperone that my ticket was with Trey, the woman barely glanced from her phone's display. Trey went in through another door, telling the chaperone there that I had both our nonexistent tickets in my purse. No one thought to bring us together and demand evidence.

We photo bombed Lindsey and Kyle's prom portrait. It was our way of saying thanks. Trey chased me around the perimeter of the dance floor. It was totally sixth grade—with lots of shouts and squeals. But then he caught me and spun me around by the waist, the skirt of my dress flowing like blue-silk waves. We requested the chicken dance and tried to get Lindsey and Kyle to dance it with us. (Only Kyle would; he's goofy like that.)

When the lights went up, Trey snagged a paper flower and some bunting, twisting and turning them until, at last, he held it out for my inspection.

"Your corsage." He bowed low and tied the monstrous thing to my wrist.

Outside, we sat on the low wall that surrounded the parking lot, the old truck taking up most of our view.

"What happens at midnight?" Trey asked.

"The carriage turns back into a pumpkin?"

"In this case, it was never *not* a pumpkin."

"Cinderella loses her shoe," I added.

He held out his legs. The toes of those men's size eleven black dress shoes caught the glow from the street lamp. "I have both of mine. You?"

I hiked up the hem of my skirt and did a little flutter kick.

After a moment, he said, "I think fairy tales have it wrong. Princesses should do more of the rescuing. They're better at it." He looked at me then, all serious dark eyes, a strand of straight black hair dipping between his brows. "I wish I'd told you what was going on."

"I wish I'd thought to ask," I confessed.

"I don't want to go home yet," he said.

"Who says we have to?"

"Doesn't the magic end at midnight?"

"Says who?"

———

THE SKY WAS the color of both the egg-shell blue fender and my dress when we pulled into the McDonald's drive-through. Trey bought us two huge coffees with the five dollar bill his uncle had given him.

"I think that was the best prom ever," he said.

"It was our only prom ever."

"I mean in the history of proms. Ours was the best prom ever."

We parked, facing the sunrise, the coffee steaming our faces. Its scent reminded me that I hadn't slept. After the first sip, I figured I wouldn't need to.

Trey sighed. "I have to work later."

"What? Really?"

"Yeah. He's letting me sleep in." He trapped his coffee cup between his legs so he could draw little air quotes around *sleep in*.

Something about the way he said those words made the coffee revolt in my stomach. For a second, I thought my egg-shell blue dress might end up egg-shell brown. Something wedged its way between us. Pride? Embarrassment? Only now did I realize we'd been living with that invisible thing all spring. I wasn't about to let it ruin this night—or all the other nights between now and forever.

"I could help," I said. "Or just hang out with you."

The coffee cup stilled halfway to his mouth. "You'd do that?"

"I might be wearing the princess dress, but I don't remember turning into one."

"You sure?" He eyed me. "I mean, the pay's lousy."

"But the company's not."

———

BY NOON, a fine layer of sawdust covered us both. It was like being in a golden-colored winter except for the sweat that stung my eyes. An impressive blister was forming on my palm. When Trey turned my hand over and inspected it, my heart thudded fast and hard. He blew on the blister, cooling my skin, then he kissed me. We stood there—under the noonday sun—sawdust turning to stardust.

Fairy tales might start with *once upon a time*. Sometimes they end with *happily ever after*. But I knew then the best fairy tales were the ones you wrote yourself.

## Speechless

ON NIGHTS BEFORE speech team practice, I dream about rodent teeth. They sprout beneath my upper lip and there's no stopping them. They grow until I'm left with not fangs, or anything vampire cool, but huge Bugs Bunny teeth. Sadly, not even in dreams do I have Bugs' way with words.

Besides, I hate carrots.

Every morning, after one of those dreams, I stand in front of the bathroom mirror, never sure what's the dream and what's the reality. With a finger, I press my front two teeth, hard. They feel naked without the braces. Four years of tasting metal. Four years of expense that could probably fund an Ivy League education. Not that I'm Ivy League bound. Not that I'm anywhere bound.

I'm the girl who never smiles in school pictures. I'm the girl who never talks. Problem is, colleges expect you to—talk that is. High test scores? AP classes? It only gets you so far. Especially when your extracurricular activities are six years of private violin lessons (*a mediocre talent who plays with more passion than skill* according to my instructor) and knitting club (Tuesdays, 7:45 a.m. in the Family and Consumer Science classroom—join us).

"You should do ... more," is what my guidance counselor suggested last time we met. Except her tone suggested it was already too late.

This is why I, Kara Blakely, the girl who never speaks, ended up on the Chisago West High speech team. Well, that, and a hot boy. Have you noticed in books and movies, and especially in real life, when a girl does something colossally stupid, there's usually some dead sexy class clown involved? Okay, maybe class clown part is just me.

Today, Jared Tomlinson (a.k.a. dead sexy class clown) isn't on my mind. Oh, I'm lying. He is. But I have a bigger problem: a new script to memorize before Saturday's speech tournament. That is, if the team coach, Mr. Ulrich, lets me swap scripts. I already know he won't be wild about the idea.

So even though it isn't my turn in front of the video camera, I freeze outside the speech team room. Despite the wall between us, their carelessly flung words pelt me through the open door. I'm bombarded with Shakespeare, Dave Barry, thoughts on the current financial crisis.

"There isn't a whole lot of funny in that," Jared Tomlinson remarks.

When it comes to the speech team, I mind the actual tournaments the least. Really. It's not like I have to check my scores or anything. I never make the final round. That leaves the whole afternoon to explore a strange high school. I might be a different girl in a strange school. I catch my reflection in the glint of trophies in their cases and think: I am a different girl.

But every Monday, I'm back where I am now. And I wonder: why does it hurt more to fail here, in front of people I've known forever than it does in front of a room full of strangers?

No one notices I'm late, not even Mr. Ulrich. The team divas, that includes Jared, surround his desk. I sit and shuffle the pages of my new script for the gazillionth time and listen while they plan Saturday's tournament strategy. This mostly revolves around Jared, who has logged firsts in extemporaneous speaking, humorous interpretation, original humor, and even poetry. Jared—the team trump card, the one Mr. Ulrich always plays to win.

Jared's a bundle of ADHD energy. Even when he sits at the back of the room, high top sneakers planted on a desk, you can tell it's taking all his effort to stay that still. His spiked blond hair is tipped with black, so it looks like he's been dipped in chocolate. He's a sugar rush boy.

He takes spectacular pratfalls in front of my locker and does this bended knee thing where he declares undying love. I always blush. I nearly smile. But I know it's a game: when he's bored, when the cheerleaders won't give him any play, he comes looking for me. I play it straight, play it silent. I'm the perfect foil, as long as I don't speak. And I don't, because someday, I hope maybe Jared will play the game for real.

At last the divas clear an adequate space around Mr. Ulrich. Without a word, I hand him my new script. He stares at me with careworn eyes. Yes, it took me forever to pick a prose piece to begin with, and here I am, changing my mind. He doesn't need me to be a problem. Silently, I promise not to be—if only. *Please. Let me switch.*

"I'm not very Dorothy Parker," I say at last, because I sense Mr. Ulrich won't let me off the hook without an explanation. It's true. I'm not. But I wish I had her courage not to care what other people think. Her sharp words sound strange coming from my mouth.

Mr. Ulrich nods. I'm glad he doesn't bullshit me, but he's also waiting for more. The phantom rabbit teeth sprout beneath my upper lip. I fight the urge to press my hand against my mouth.

"This piece is more like me," I say. Quiet. Somber. It's from *A Testament of Youth* by Vera Brittain, about the First World War.

Mr. Ulrich looks halfway interested. He leafs through the script. The breeze from the pages touches my face. "Write an introduction tying it to the conflict in Afghanistan and you might—" Here, he pauses. His scrutiny makes me hyperaware of my teeth. "You might just have something."

I can't believe those words. I want confirmation. I want Mr. Ulrich to elaborate. But before I can ask, Jared leans all the way across Mr. Ulrich's desk, simply because he can, like everything on the speech team is his business.

"You change scripts like I change underwear," he says.

Mr. Ulrich rolls his eyes and turns to another student. My cheeks burn. Now I'll never know what he meant.

"Well," I snap at Jared. "That isn't saying much, is it?"

These aren't words I actually thought, never mind planned on saying. They came from nowhere and now I can't take them back. Jared stares, his mouth an O of incomprehension. I've broken something, shattered it. Something I never knew we shared. I grab my might-have-something script and bolt.

In the girls' bathroom, I'm at the mirror, finger pressed hard against my two front teeth. The relief of that floods me. I'm almost dizzy with it. I'm there, nose pressed against the glass, taking deep breaths when Jared walks in. Just like that. Into the girls' bathroom. Heat explodes in my cheeks, but I don't turn around.

"What are you doing?" he asks.

Our gazes touch in the mirror's reflection. I press a protective finger against my teeth.

"Don't," he says. "You have a beautiful mouth."

I can't remove my finger, so I squeeze my eyes shut. I stay like that until Jared's high tops squeak against the tile floor and his footsteps fade down the hall.

---

I BLINK. The girl in the glint of a strange trophy blinks back. It's Saturday afternoon; I'm done for the day; and my armpits are nearly dry after three preliminary prose rounds. The lobby is empty, so I pluck at my blouse to get a breeze going. A month ago, Mom bought me some vanilla chai deodorant. At the time, I thought it was cool. Now I worry that I smell like a Starbucks.

But this school? Doesn't smell at all. The speech tournament is being held at the richest high school in the richest suburb of the Twin Cities. The lobby is a mausoleum of glass and trophies. Chisago, Minnesota isn't small, but our school smells like books and sneakers and sweat, and our trophies don't glow quite as bright.

I blink again. This time, when I open my eyes, Jared Tomlinson stands behind me. He's golden in the surface of a trophy (some football thing) and so quiet. No bended knee action, no ADHD bouncing. If I'm a different girl, then maybe he's a different boy.

"You headed for the prose finals?" he asks.

Different isn't always good. He knows I'm not. He knows I never make the final round. The whole team knows that. I shake my head.

"For real? I mean, did you check your scores?"

I decide golden Jared has too much tarnish, so I turn to face the real one. "You don't have to do this," I say. The phantom rabbit teeth haunt me. It's all I can do not to press a finger against my upper lip. "I'm sorry about the other day."

The briefest of smiles tips one corner of his mouth. "You're pretty funny."

"I'm not—"

"And I got served." He pulls at a strand of hair as if inspecting the tip for its chocolate coating. "Next time, I'll know to expect it."

Next time? I have twelve inappropriate thoughts all at once, all about Jared. I remind myself that I am not that golden trophy girl.

"So," he says. "Prose finals. Can I walk you there? It's right across the hall from humorous interp."

Which is where Jared is headed. The tournament where Jared Tomlinson doesn't final is the one he doesn't attend. He's staring at me with eyes that match his chocolate-dipped hair. I know: he won't let me go until I say it.

"I didn't make the finals."

He rocks on his heels, hands clasped behind his back. The whole purpose of this conversation starts to sink in. Heat blooms under my arms. I'm hot enough to boil the deodorant off my skin. I'm a latte girl. Pour me into a paper cup and call it done.

He checked the scores. That's clear now. Checked, and then came looking for me. Talk about getting served. A heaping dish of cold revenge to go along with my hot latte self.

"You know I didn't make the finals," I say again.

"Well, okay. Maybe," he says. "But can I ask you something?"

"What?"

"Would you like to?"

———

JARED DOESN'T SPEAK to me anymore. Not in the hallways, the speech team room, and never at tournaments. On Thursday afternoons, I sneak up to the third floor. Physically, it's about as far away from the speech team room as you can get. In a small classroom that I think was a storage closet at one time, except it has windows, Jared is always waiting. How he gets there first, I don't know, but he always does.

He sits in back, high tops on a desk. I stand up front and read my piece over and over and over again. Somehow, when it's me and Jared, it's worse, worse than taking my turn in front of the video camera. I remind myself that the true worst case scenario can never happen. I'll never end up competing against Jared.

This fact makes reading for Jared easier. And reading is key. Judges mark you down if you sound like you've memorized your script, even if we all have. When I blow a line or a paragraph, stumble over a word I've read a hundred times, I feel my teeth. Big, fat, rabbit fangs I can't talk around.

"You're doing it again," he complains.

I freeze. "What?"

"Hiding." His high tops clomp to the floor. He pushes himself up like this is the most arduous thing he's done all day. He reaches the front of the room and presses the top of my script. It inches lower, then higher as I resist, then lower when I give up.

"Trust me," he says. "If the judges can't see your face, they'll rank you lower."

I don't bother reminding Jared I'm always ranked lowest. On a scale of one (the best) to five (the worst), I've never even earned a four. I start reading again, and again he rushes to the front of the room.

He eases the script lower and asks, "Why?"

"Why what?" I ask, although I know what he means.

"You hide."

I shake my head.

"Not your face." He raises a hand. "But your mouth." His fingertips come to rest on my lower lip.

It's all I can do not to flinch, to run away. The rabbit teeth sprout, grow to epic proportion. Huge, hideous. I know they're there. I feel them. From the way Jared stares, I can tell he doesn't see them. Worse, from the way he stares, I can't tell what he sees.

He leans in. Some unseen force tugs me closer. I'm gripping the script so hard, the paper crinkles, and then our bodies crush it. A spike of that chocolate-dipped hair grazes my forehead a second before Jared kisses me.

I open my mouth, to warn him about the rabbit teeth, and his tongue touches mine. I feel my eyes widen, but Jared has his closed, so I do the same. He kisses me and doesn't stop. I'm amazed at how he can make my mouth feel petite, dainty, yet endless all at once.

At last he pulls away, rests his forehead against mine. Beneath the skin of his neck, his pulse beats wildly.

"You have a beautiful mouth," he says before stepping back.

I'm chilled from where my body met his, from where his lips touched mine. I want to press my fingers against that wildly beating pulse, but I can't let go of my crushed script. I want him to kiss me again, but I can't find the words to say so.

"Read for me?" he says.

I nod. It's all I can do.

Jared says it's my best reading yet. I take his word for it because I can't remember uttering a single sentence. Afterward, we leave like we always do, Jared first.

"Just give me a minute," he says, but I give him more.

I stand at the windows overlooking the parking lot and wait until he bursts through the front double doors of the school. I wonder about the boy who coaches me, kisses me, but doesn't want to be seen with me. At the thought, my index finger moves toward my two front teeth, but I stop it, clutch both my hands together.

With my forehead against the cool glass, I watch Jared drive away.

————

JARED MAKES me check my scores. Every tournament. And while officially we never speak to each other, except for a casual hello or whatever, he'll text me relentlessly until I send my scores back to him. I can't make anything up, either, because I know he's already checked

I also attend final rounds, as a spectator. Sometimes I sit in on Jared's, but he's hard to find. Mr. Ulrich shuffles him from category to category—at the last minute if the tournament rules allow it—all in the quest for a slot at the state tournament. Jared's been twice. This year, Mr. Ulrich wants him to win.

I still inspect the trophies in each school's lobby. You can tell a lot from what a school has and how they show it off. But now, I sit in the auditorium with the speech team for the awards ceremony. I'm pretty sure no one notices when I clap the hardest for Jared.

"A two," he says to me on Monday. He's sitting at the desk in front of mine, a copy of *Best American Short Stories 2005* in his hands. Of course, it's upside down. This is a game to see how long I, or someone else on the team, can go without mentioning it. The book is our camouflage, so one notices our conversation.

"Two, three, four," he lists off my scores. "What do you call that? A straight flush?"

"I don't play poker," I say.

"But you gamble."

I don't have an answer for that. Briefly, I touch my tongue to my teeth. They feel smaller today, but then it's not my turn in front of the video camera. Those slots are taken by the kids sweating for the regional tournament, set for next Saturday.

"You're ready," Jared says.

"For what?"

"The final round."

My stomach tightens at the thought, but I force a laugh. "Maybe next year."

"No." And he says this last quietly. "Next week."

Despite my scores, much improved, I'm not ready for regionals. The top three from each final round move on to state. That's Jared territory, team diva territory. It's golden trophy girl territory, but it's not me.

"The thing about regionals," Jared says, "is anything can happen." He nods toward the front of the room. Under the video camera's lens, Will—Jared's best friend and sometime rival in humorous interpretation—melts. I want to take a tissue and wipe away the moisture that mixes with the peach fuzz on his upper lip. I want to tell him I understand.

But Jared, sitting in front of me, isn't sweating. He stares at me, willing something from me. A yes, a nod, anything. All I can do is pull my upper lip over my teeth and bite the flesh, not enough to draw blood, but enough to earn Jared's frown.

"Regionals," he repeats and the word is starting to lose its meaning. "You. Are. Ready."

I close my eyes and swallow back the fear. I can't decide if I hope Jared is right or wrong.

———

I AM LATTE GIRL. I conquer my opponents, not with strength, but with the subliminal suggestion they must flee to the nearest Starbucks for something hot and over-priced. Actually, all I've done is wear a vest I made during knitting club over my usual boring white blouse. The layers, combined with the deodorant, make me a vanilla chai latte, extra hot.

I haven't checked my scores. Jared hasn't texted me. That, all by itself, is weird. I even hide in a far lobby corner and pull out my phone, making sure the battery hasn't died, making sure I didn't miss a message. It hasn't. I didn't.

I wonder how bad my scores are. The preliminary rounds are a blur. I remember standing in front of the room; I remember sitting at my desk afterward. The rest is a jumble of words.

Down the hall, a crowd surrounds the posted scores for each category. A few squeals echo. A few guys bump fists. A few others huddle in the corridor, going over notes. And a fair number look both disappointed and relieved.

My hand clenches the phone in my skirt pocket. I purse my lips, but my teeth feel normal, or almost so. I ease my way through the throng. I collect stares, but I glance away, not wanting to see the pity. I scan the prose interpretation list for my name. Blakely is near the top.

3, 1, 1

I freeze, wondering if another Blakely, Kara competed today. The three makes sense. Two girls in my first round were excellent. But the other two scores? First, in two rounds. It doesn't seem possible. I inch toward the other posted list, the one that tells the finalists the time and place for the final round. It's a list I've never bothered to check. It's a list that has my name on it.

It's also a list where the name Tomlinson, Jared appears below mine.

I spin, knocking into one of the girls from my first round, a girl who has also made the prose finals. Like me. Like Jared.

"Congrats," she says. Despite the old fashioned librarian bun and narrow rimmed glasses, she looks like she just sashayed off the cheerleading squad. "You were great."

"You, too," I manage with an exhale.

"See you in the finals." She grins and walks away.

"Sure," I say, although her back is now turned. I'm still fighting for air, for some sense of reality. I have neither when Mr. Ulrich finds me.

"Kara," he says. "I can't tell you how impressed I am with your progress this year."

My throat dry, my lungs empty, I nod.

"I know it's early yet, but next year, I want you to consider poetry. Think about it over the summer. Do some reading." When I don't say anything, he adds, "I'd sit in on the final round, but I'm judging dramatic inter-pretation."

He leaves without wishing me luck. What would be

the point to that? I'm already a lucky hand, a fluke. Jared's the ace up his sleeve. *Jared*. I still haven't seen him. I know I won't until I walk into classroom 27 for the final round.

———

JARED SITS at a desk in the very back of the room. Our gazes touch when I walk in. I see questioning there, get a sense of pleading. I break eye contact, wishing I could do more, wishing I could shatter it, never look at Jared again. I pick a desk at the front, diagonal from him. To look at him, I have to twist around. I won't do that.

The fog of making the finals, of seeing Jared's name on the prose list finally clears. Now I see all the deliberate moves in this game. I wonder. If I had just remained silent the day I asked Mr. Ulrich if I could switch pieces. If I'd been what I'd always been—speechless—I wouldn't be sitting here.

I feel trapped in my boring white blouse, hot in my knitted vest. The scent of vanilla chai reaches me and my stomach churns. After all this time, I finally understand the boy who coaches me, kisses me, but doesn't want to be seen with me. Or think I do. Five minutes before the round starts, Jared stands next to my desk.

"Kara." His whisper is urgent, almost fierce.

I glare up at him.

"I'm sorry," he says. "I wanted to tell you, explain that it wasn't … I mean, it wasn't about you. But more about me, and state, and I'm just so sick of—"

More words follow, but I key in on their sound, the feeling behind them. If I didn't know better, I'd say Jared hates speech team. A new version of the game plays in my head, one just as deliberate, but one that isn't really about me.

"What I'm trying to say is—" He sounds like he's drowning.

"Don't." No. It's not about me at all. I think the thoughts slowly. It's about Jared. "Don't you dare throw the final round."

He shakes his head, but I see the answer in his eyes. That has been his plan all along, to throw the final round, to *not* go to state. I don't understand why; I don't have time, or the courage, to ask. Before either of us can say another word, the judge enters the room.

The final round begins.

I read second, the perfect slot. No jitters about being the first, no angst in waiting. My voice shakes on the first few lines. It's not my best reading, but something tells me it's not my worst, either.

Jared follows my piece with one from Tim O'Brien's *The Things They Carried*, about Vietnam. Even this feels orchestrated, like I've merely set the stage for him. The dead sexy class clown can do serious. And he does. He's perfectly serious. If there were such a thing as perfectly perfect, he'd be that too. This doesn't surprise me. I'm not surprised, either, when the cheerleader librarian blows us all out of the water with her excerpt from *The Prime of Miss Jean Brodie*.

When the round ends, I rush to the girls' bathroom. Today, I know, Jared won't follow. I splash water on my face. I take deep breaths. Amazingly, I almost forget my teeth. In fact, I have forgotten them. It's an afterthought, the force of habit that has me touching a finger to them. But I don't press and a moment later, drop my hand. I smile at myself instead.

During the awards ceremony, Will struts across the stage to accept first in humorous interpretation. He raises the trophy high above his head. All of us on the Chisago team overwhelm the auditorium with our cheers. After that, I slip out. I haven't inspected this school's trophies, at least, not closely. Somehow, that seems more important than the ranking for prose interpretation.

I already know I'm not going to state. I already know Jared is. Mr. Ulrich can accept my honorable mention ribbon. After all, this is his game.

Basketball is this school's sport. In fact, I can't find a single football trophy, not even a token one. The boys here must be skinny giants, with endlessly long limbs. I bet they're sweaty too. I wonder if they'd like to borrow my vanilla chai deodorant. I catch the image of the golden trophy girl and she laughs.

"Kara?"

I didn't hear him approach, but I sense him now, a wave of that ADHD energy rolling off him. I consider not turning, but figure the golden trophy girl would face Jared. If she can, then so can I.

He's holding a second place trophy in one hand, an honorable mention ribbon in the other.

"I'm sorry," he says. "I—"

"Congrats," I say, trying to sound like that golden trophy girl, or maybe the cheerleader librarian. "Good luck at state."

"Please, Kara, the thing is—"

"I don't care what the thing is." Honestly, I don't. Or at least, not much.

"Let me explain?" Jared pleads. He hefts the trophy and lets the ribbon flutter. "One of these is yours. Don't you want to know which one?"

I let my previous answer hang in the air. I don't care. Well, not a hundred percent anyway. Despite this, Jared has my attention.

"It's your fault, you know," he says. "That piece you picked to read. It gave Mr. Ulrich an idea."

"Oh, sure. Blame me." I can tell by the way Jared's mouth turns up, that it sounds funny, that he still thinks I'm funny.

"He wanted both me and Will at state, and he thought I had a better chance at serious than Will." He rubs his hair and I'm almost surprised that he doesn't wipe away the chocolate tips. "Even the piece was his idea, or really, in a way, it was yours. That's why I started coaching you, and why we couldn't tell anyone. I didn't think what Ulrich was doing was fair. And I thought ..."

He trails off and now, he really does have my attention. I don't care about the trophy or the ribbon, but I'll combust into chai-scented flames if he won't tell me more.

"I thought you had a chance," he says, at last. "So what if you hadn't been on the team before? I wanted to prove that with actual coaching, anyone could."

"Even me." I'm not a golden trophy girl. I'm a science experiment.

"Especially you. You're good. You might even be a

natural at this. First year, and look." He holds out the awards at arm's length. "One of these is yours."

I step forward, put a hand on each of his, and gently push the trophy and the ribbon so they rest against his chest. "No. They're both yours."

"I'm tired of always winning," he says.

I wonder, if after a while, it loses meaning. The award becomes the expectation. The award becomes something you resent.

"And I'm tired of—" he breaks off, stares hard at the trophy.

"Of being used," I finish for him.

If gratitude were a drink, I'd never go thirsty. It rolls off Jared, sweet, hot, and way better than Starbucks.

"Thank you for not throwing the final round," I say. "I don't want to win that way."

"Who says you didn't?" He hands me the trophy.

I don't believe it. Not for a second. I refuse to take it from him. "This isn't mine."

He sets it, and the ribbon, at my feet. "Okay, maybe not. But can I ask you something?"

"What?"

"Would you like it to be?" He turns, not waiting for my answer, and heads down the hall.

I stare at the trophy on the linoleum, at the ones in the cases that surround me in this strange school's lobby. I catch sight of golden Jared fading away, and golden trophy girl, reaching a hand toward him.

"Jared?"

He freezes, but doesn't turn around. I glance at trophy girl again and, I swear, she winks.

"When do we start?"

And his kiss? That's better than Starbucks too. This time, when I open my mouth, I think it's Jared who's surprised.

*Speechless* was first published online as part of the launch for *The Geek Girl's Guide to Cheerleading*, April 2009

## Breaking Plans

THE DAY I UNDERSTOOD why we hid the Bacardi bottles at the bottom of the recycling bin, I stopped fighting my Aunt Jenny. She urged me forward—her hopes like soft fingertips against the small of my back—into enrichment courses I loathed, into summer school classes I resented, into anything that would take me from here to somewhere else.

It worked. Even in kindergarten, I remembered thinking: *someday I will leave.* Life—or at least, my life—started after high school. I had plans, and no one was going to change that.

But today, after last bell, someone did.

When I saw Simon Lansky standing outside the detention room, my heart sped up. Sure, detention was my only extracurricular, but it was never his. Here was a kid who would only get a wrist slap for robbing a bank. He was just too, too … well, Simon Lansky, with the cuffs of his jeans that skimmed his ankles, shirts that were perpetually half-tucked in, blond hair neither straight nor curly. It looked like a wheat field after a windstorm, the stalks blown this way or that. He was the go-to guy whenever the varsity cheerleaders needed a fool for a pep rally skit. Last year, the synchronized swim team dumped him into the pool at the end of their exhibition show—rented tux and all. Simon was the sort of boy who wore bunny slippers on pajama day. He was not the sort of boy who stood outside the detention room, ever.

"Hey, Constance," he said, as if detention was our thing.

"Hey, yourself." Truth was, he was also my go-to guy. Whenever I needed a lab partner for honors physics or a work partner in an AP class, I never had to look to him. He was already there.

His gaze darted to the room's interior, then back to me. "You still doing this?"

I shrugged. Did it matter? On the other side of the country, a scholarship and a work-study program waited for me at a small, liberal arts college—one that viewed my detention record more as a charming quirk than a liability. "What else am I going to do?"

"Oh, I don't know," he said, sounding cagey. "Shop for a dress?"

"A ... dress?"

Simon grinned. If his hair resembled a wheat field, then his eyes were the perfect blue sky above it. "You know," he added, "to wear to prom."

From inside the room came a snicker.

I pushed one word past my suddenly dry lips. "Prom?"

"Ever been?"

"No. Never planned on it, either."

"Well, plans were made to be broken."

"I thought that was rules."

"You already break enough of those," he said. "So, what do you say?"

That snicker again. My cheeks stung. Simon stood there, like he hadn't heard the laughter. He was too, too … Simon Lansky for that.

"Sure," I said, my voice silencing everyone in detention. "I'll go to prom with you."

————

HERE'S the thing about my mom: she doesn't always drink. Months can pass without the aroma of rum seeping into the walls of our apartment. But when she drinks? Well, she *drinks*. Long and hard, like rum is the only thing keeping her alive, like rum is the only reason she lives. The summer I was fourteen, I painted my room three separate times because the fumes from *Biscay Blue* smothered those from the bottle.

Now, a silent mantra played in my head: *please don't drink on prom day, one day, one dress, one dance.* I owed Simon that much.

Thing was, I'd been shopping with Mom when our third, silent companion had been a silver hip flask. I owned a closet full of things bought under the influence. I'd stopped having friends over long ago. Actually, I'd stopped having friends, period. Real life could start once I had a diploma and two thousand miles between me and her.

So naturally, on the morning of prom, when I

wandered into the kitchen, Mom was knocking back her first Bacardi and Diet Coke. I shot a look at Aunt Jenny. I brought my hands together. *Please. Do something.*

"Sylvia?" Aunt Jenny said, expertly slipping the glass from Mom's hand. "This day means a lot to Constance."

Actually, it didn't, but I wasn't going to argue the finer points.

"I'm just so excited." Mom reached for me. I let my feet cement to the floor and refused to move. "Prom!" Mom continued, pretending not to notice my stance. "It's so hard to believe."

I almost rolled my eyes at that.

"I just needed a little something to calm my nerves."

In a stealth move, Aunt Jenny slipped me the Bacardi bottle, and I slipped outside with it. I drained it fully before tossing the thing into the recycling bin. When I returned to the kitchen, Aunt Jenny was talking in her *bright, everything's okay* voice.

"So, what do you two say? Fremont Mall or do we make the trek to Mall of America?"

Mom: "Mall of America!"

Me: "Why don't you just shoot me?"

"Fremont Mall it is," Aunt Jenny said, clasping her hands together. Under her breath, she added, "You'll be gone in less than six months." In her tone, I caught her silent plea:

*Let me have this. Let your mother have this.*

---

"OH, HONESTLY, CONSTANCE." Aunt Jenny held up a

sequins dress that was both slutty and frumpy—and so shiny, it could double as an emergency reflective blanket, for an infant. "There's nothing on the racks. We should've done this weeks ago."

Of course, *weeks ago*, I didn't have plans for prom.

"Honey, look what I found!" Mom burst through the racks of clearance dresses—last year's prom castoffs, failed formals, and hopeless homecoming gowns—with something beige slung over her arm.

Beige. *God*. She'd started drinking again.

"It was over in the hoity-toity section, but look. I think it's perfect for our baby." She shook out the dress and the skirt flowed like cream. Then she held it up against me.

Aunt Jenny stared, mouth half open. I turned slowly, reluctantly, toward the tri-fold mirrors. With barely a glance, I calculated the dress's potential. Normally, I'm a Dr. Martin, kohl eyeliner, ripped jeans kind of girl. But this? This was amazing. It put all the dresses in the junior department to shame. It reminded me of those black and white movies Mom and Aunt Jenny watched when I was little—after the divorces but before the drinking. Maybe that was why Mom picked it. Maybe she wanted to remind me of that, or remember it herself.

She pressed the gown into my arms and spun me toward the changing rooms. "Try it on." Her whisper touched my ear and brushed my cheek. I caught a hint of toothpaste. My stomach clenched as I braced for what always came next: that telltale hint of alcohol.

I was in the changing room before I realized the mint on her breath hadn't been laced with rum.

———

THING WAS, the logic of Simon dragging me to anything that involved a prom committee escaped me. What was he trying to prove? That it was possible for me to make nice with the in-crowd? Some grand science experiment to prove our animosity wasn't an integral part of our genetic code? (My pet theory, actually.)

I stood five foot ten in sneakers, but when we walked into the college ballroom on Saturday afternoon, my insides shriveled. Then Simon grabbed my hand and squeezed it.

"Everyone here knows Constance, right?" His jeans were too short—again. His shirt? Best described as disaster in plaid. But every last one of the mean-girl brigade gave him a toothy smile. This was what happened when you saved someone's ass repeatedly and so publically.

They owed you. And today? Today, Simon was cashing in.

"She's here to help," he added as if only I could provide the perfect finishing touch to the crepe paper decorations.

Apparently, he believed that. He loaded me down with oversized paper flowers and instructions to top off lovers' lane.

"They're awful," I said before he had a chance to walk away.

"It wouldn't be prom without large, hideous paper flowers."

I rattled my armful of crepe paper. "I don't mean these."

His gaze went to a cluster of girls whose whispers clouded the air. "Yeah. They are. The world is full of awful people." He shrugged. "Why not make it a little bit better."

"With paper flowers?"

"Exactly." He spun me by the shoulders and aimed me at lovers' lane.

I lugged flowers down the lane, stopping every foot or so to reach up on tiptoe to staple one to the top of the chicken wire. The flowers hid most of the lane's skeletal understructure. The peach and azure weren't quite so hideous when not right in your face. In fact, they were perfect for showing off my dress.

I was contemplating this, and hoping the band wouldn't be totally lame, when hissed words filtered through the crepe paper and into my thoughts.

"*Gawd*, can you believe he asked her? I thought you'd fix him up with someone decent."

"*Please*. Up until two weeks ago, I thought he was gay."

"Oh, of course," the first girl said. "It's a pity date."

My insides clenched, from toes to stomach to head. My brain shrank so small, I couldn't think, my throat so tight, I couldn't swallow. Only my eyes felt bigger—and wetter.

"Simon's always doing stuff like that," she continued. "Remember when he dressed up in a pony costume for McKayla's horse rescue fundraiser?"

That made me what? Just another project to make the world a little less awful? Was I … awful? He'd always been my go-to guy, but what did that make me? My fingers squeezed the stapler and I shot off a few staples. They plinked against the ballroom floor. I sucked in a breath, certain the girls on the other side had heard.

They continued to drone, their voices buzzing in my ears, words indistinct. I was still standing there in lover's lane, stapler clasped in my hand when Simon came to drive me home.

———

I THOUGHT about slicing the beige dress to shreds, grabbing the kitchen shears—the blades encrusted from years of cutting frozen entrée containers—and going all *Psycho* on the thing.

Then the charge on Aunt Jenny's credit card flashed into my mind. I'd wear the dress—and I'd look damn good in it too—but Simon's prom was not going to go according to plan, at least, not any of his plans. He wanted awful? Well, I'd show him awful.

When the doorbell rang, Aunt Jenny shoved me into the kitchen, insisting I needed to make a grand entrance. Yes. From the kitchen.

"What you need is a staircase," Mom observed, drily, in more ways than one. If there was a rum bottle in the house, neither Aunt Jenny, I—nor possibly Mom—knew about it. "You can't sweep into a room without a staircase."

From the living room came Aunt Jenny's singsong of: "Constance! Someone's here to see you!"

Like Simon's arrival was a surprise. I rolled my eyes at Mom and she giggled.

"You'll be okay tonight?" I said.

"We're streaming *Casablanca* and *The Philadelphia Story*. Go have fun. We'll be fine."

I made my grand entrance. Simon stopped speaking mid-sentence. His mouth went slack. The hand that held a plastic corsage box fell to his side. To his credit, he didn't drop the flowers.

"Wow." He turned to Aunt Jenny. "I didn't know it would look like that."

"I sent him a picture," Aunt Jenny said.

"So I could do this." He hiked up a black trouser leg to expose a beige sock, the exact gentle cream of my dress.

I studied Simon in his tux. The trousers? A little too short. All the better to see the beige socks, I supposed. The jacket? A little snug across the shoulders and the sleeves hit him just above the wrists.

"That isn't what I think it is," I said. "Is it?"

"Yeah, from last year. After it ended up in the pool, the tux place didn't want it back and sold it to me at a discount. I was all set until I grew another inch. But hey!" He waved a beige ankle at me. "Now I get to do this."

My resolve softened under the heat of Simon's relentless cheer. Did nothing get this boy down? Not even paying for a tux someone else ruined? I stood there, shaking my head, when Aunt Jenny called out, "Pictures!" again in singsong.

My mouth felt numb, but I forced a smile. I tried to ignore how nice Simon's hip felt against mine, his fingertips on the small of my back. The camera's flash blinded me and I used that as an excuse to turn away and hide my face.

———

"I HOPE YOU DON'T MIND," Simon said as I navigated concrete steps in strappy gold sandals. "I promised my mom we'd stop by for pictures." He pulled out his phone and aimed it in my direction. "I told her I'd take a bunch, but that's not good enough."

The phone clicked while Simon documented my descent.

"Those are keepers," I said.

"This one of your foot is particularly nice." He punched a few more buttons and my foot became his phone's wallpaper.

"You're a nut."

"It's why you're going to prom with me."

There went my resolve again, slipping right through my fingers. I needed to get my bitch on, and I needed to do it now.

The minivan stopped me.

Not that we were going to prom in one. I didn't know much about Simon's home life, but I was glad he didn't go into debt renting a limo. But something about the minivan was … odd, in a way I couldn't put my finger on.

"Hope you don't mind." Simon rushed to open the door for me. "We got it a few months ago. Man, that new car smell is something else." He flung open the door, then took my hand to help me inside.

The minivan was the kind with three rows of seats. Except. One row was missing. Instead, there was a folded ramp and space for a wheelchair. I couldn't stop staring at the nonexistent seats. The space seemed too large and, at the same time, insubstantial.

"Lifesaver," Simon said, nodding at the emptiness. "Now my mom can get him to his doctor appointments, and they can actually go places, too."

*Him.* I didn't ask.

When we reached his house, a pack of kids spilled out onto the front porch, followed by a woman who had the same blue eyes as Simon. Three of the smallest threw their arms around Simon's legs while the rest bounced and raced around the minivan.

"Sorry," the woman called. "I tried to stop them. You'd think they were the ones going to prom." She looked like someone who'd lunch at the country club—except for the plaid shirt, the jeans that were just a bit too short, and the dishtowel still in her hands.

"Mom," Simon said. "This is Constance." He turned toward me. "Constance, this is my mom. Usually she doesn't carry a dishtowel."

She glanced at the towel, grinned, then extended her hand. "Mara Lansky."

I'd never had a boyfriend long enough to run the gauntlet of meeting the parents, but I liked Mara Lansky immediately. I liked that she shook my hand.

"Come inside," she said.

The kids scrambled up the ramp next to the porch steps, the screech and clang of the screen door echoing behind them. Simon nodded toward the house.

"It's not as scary as it looks," he said.

"It is when you're an only child."

Mara laughed. "Fortunately, only some of them are mine."

Simon took my hand and led me up the steps. "I want you to meet my dad."

And just like that, he put words to my true hesitation.

————

THE LANSKY'S living room felt cramped, like I had to duck my head. Furniture was shoved so close together only the smallest Lansky could squeeze between an arm of the sofa and a chair. In my heels, I towered over everything—except Simon. Mara Lansky posed us by the fireplace, its mantel covered with photos, certificates, drawings.

I heard the whoosh before comprehending what it must be. I saw the wheels first, then the chair came into view. My vision tunneled, then expanded to take in bits and pieces all at once. A photo on the mantel of a man in uniform, brown earth extending for miles behind him. Iraq or Afghanistan? I knew I'd never ask. A National Merit Scholarship certificate with Simon's name. A wedding photo. Simon as a baby, dressed all in blue to match his eyes.

I swayed, the heels of my shoes threatening to snap beneath me. I was saved by Simon's very calm, very reassuring voice.

"Hey, Dad. This is Constance."

"Your prom date?" Mr. Lansky shook his head in mock disbelief. He had the same tousled wheat field hair as Simon. "I don't know, son. I think she might be out of your league."

I felt a pinprick against my cheeks, the impulse to run urging me toward the door. I clutched the skirt of my dress, the silky material cooling my palm. I strode across the room. I stuck out my hand.

"It's nice to meet you, sir." I'd never called anyone *sir* before. It wasn't happening again anytime soon, either. But in that moment, it felt right. Right, but not enough, so I added, "Your son is the most wonderful person I know."

———

THE REMAINING TIME at Simon's went by in an explosion of camera flashes and little kid screeches. In the car, he turned to me and asked:

"What's wrong?"

*I was.* The words wouldn't leave my mouth, so I shook my head and tried to smile.

"Yeah, they can wear out anyone. Why do you think I spend so much time at school?"

It was ten thirty when Simon led me to a table, one abandoned by the jocks, their cheerleaders, the horse-rescuing McKayla, and all the girls from the prom committee. Plastic cups half-filled with punch dotted the table, the aroma more illicit alcohol than tropical fruit.

"Ugh." I wrinkled my nose. "They really *are* awful."

Simon snorted and helped me clear the space.

"You okay?" he asked.

"I feel a little shell-shocked." I regretted the phrase the second it hit the air. But if Simon noticed my poor choice of words, he didn't say.

Instead, he asked, "Do you remember that pep rally in ninth grade, where they gave away all those MP3 players and the laptop?"

Amazingly, I did. Maybe it was the amount of stuff one of the local businesses was giving away. Maybe it was because I'd longed for (and didn't win) the laptop. "Didn't you win something?"

"A music player. Do you remember what happened after they called my name?"

I shook my head, trying to conjure up something more than the aftertaste of disappointment of not winning something myself.

"My shoelaces were untied," he continued. "I did a face-plant in the middle of the gymnasium floor."

In front of the whole school. Of course. He'd come by his reputation as pep rally fool honestly.

"I was only down for about five seconds, but I remember thinking: I could let this define everything that happens to me in high school, or I could use it to my advantage."

I planted my elbow on the table and propped my chin on my hand, looking for guile in those innocent blue eyes. Just how self-aware was Simon?

"And you don't mind?"

He shrugged. "What's to mind?"

"For starters, how about having to pay for a pool-soaked tux?" Or dressing up like a horse's ass, or whatever humiliating thing the cheerleading squad made him do.

"Small price."

"For what?"

74

"Doing whatever I like. Having fun."

"High school isn't fun."

"Well, not for you." His tone said: *That's your own fault.*

Maybe it was. But there was nothing here in this school—in this town—that I really cared about.

"And what about you?" he asked a moment later.

"What about me?"

"This isn't zombie prom, but I've been dancing with one all night."

True. Only now was my head beginning to clear, no thanks to the alcohol fumes.

"I was going to ruin your prom," I confessed.

"Honestly? You're doing a bang up job of that."

"I mean, I was going to—" What was it the guidance counselor always said? "—act out."

"That would've been more fun," he said. "Actually, I was kind of hoping you would. So what happened?"

"I met your family."

I'd never seen someone deflate before, but Simon did, like I'd stuck a pin in him and everything imploded.

"It's funny," he said. "I thought, of anyone, you'd understand."

"What?"

"Wanting to escape."

Yeah. I should have.

He gave me a smile and until that moment, I never realized how much sadness lay underneath. He shook his head, a single, dismissive gesture, and his gaze took in the ballroom as if he were saying goodbye to all that.

"Let's go," was all he said.

A hot, tight knot formed in my stomach. Well, I'd

wanted to ruin Simon's prom, hadn't I? That was the plan. I'd managed to execute it flawlessly. We stood and crossed the ballroom floor.

For the first time that night, Simon didn't take my hand.

———

OUTSIDE, in the common area, water danced through colored lights in the fountain—our school colors, in fact, blue and gold. It was totally cheesy, but I stood there, my gaze following streams of water from spout to crest, and back into the pool.

"Constance?" Simon paused a few feet ahead of me. His voice sounded tired, like the weight of the world resided in his pockets.

I didn't want to leave, which was funny because I could count the days—the hours—until I left this town, left everything I hated about it. Except. I didn't hate everything. Or everyone.

I reached down and undid the strap of my sandal.

"Constance, come on."

I undid the other strap.

"What are you doing?"

I kicked off the sandals. "Acting out."

Skirt gathered in my arms, I eased one foot and then the other into the pool.

"How is it?" Simon called.

"Like they dumped a hundred trays of ice cubes in here."

"That good?"

The cold numbed my toes, my skin puckering in a thousand goose bumps. After a moment, a splash sounded behind me. Simon slogged his way toward me, not even bothering to roll the legs of his pants.

"Yeah." He scooped a handful of water and let it rain on the sleeve of his tux. "Like this is going to make it worse." His damp hands caught mine. I let go of my dress, and it plummeted until the skirt floated on the blue and gold froth.

"I don't want to leave," I said.

"If you don't, how can I live vicariously through you?"

I'd meant prom. But maybe it was more than that. It was only as I was poised to walk out the door that I discovered a reason to stay—a reason that was here all along.

"But in the fall," I began, "you'll be—"

"Getting a job, taking some night classes."

I thought about that National Merit Scholarship certificate. I thought about fathers in wheelchairs and moms who hid bottles of rum. I thought about all the things we couldn't run away from—and all the things we could run toward.

"I'll miss you," I said.

"Good."

He pulled me close, like he never wanted to let me go, but his fingertips pressed into the small of my back, urging me forward.

It felt like hope.

# PART II

## Later

### TALES OF THE FUTURE AND FANTASTIC

## Just a Matter of Time

To: Sadie.Lin@email.com
From: TimeThief@email.com
Subject: You're running out of time

If time is money, then someone is robbing you blind.

A Friend

WHEN THE MESSAGE landed in my inbox, from a fake account, I ignored it. It was spam. Or a joke. Or one of those random things that happen on the Internet—and if you fell into that time suck, then you deserved to get robbed.

So I deleted it and went back to AP World History.

But two weeks later, as I sat in the orchestra room, my hand clutched the neck of my violin like I might strangle it. I wondered if I really had run out of time—or become very bad at managing it. I'd been late for tonight's special practice. I let the violin strings bite into my fingers, preferring pain to shame.

I blinked, trying to figure out when the room had cleared. I blinked again as if waking from a dream and breathed in the stale, silent air. I looked from my own hands, still clutching the violin, to the ones on the clock.

6:38.

The fire of lost time started in my toes, raced up my legs and straight to my heart. I jumped. My music stand crashed into the director's podium, but I didn't bother to right it. In the storage room, my fingers fumbled with the closures to my violin case. I had everything locked in the cubby, but when I turned to leave, I nearly crushed my bow beneath the sole of my ballet flat. More wasted time.

Bow tucked away, I sprinted to the lobby, fear like a fist in my stomach. The significance of the closed auditorium doors slammed into me—and me into them. The thud echoed, then died. Above me, the clock read:

7:00.

Muted applause reached me from behind the closed doors. A name echoed, one that sounded a lot like *Sadie Lin*. Somehow I'd missed the start of the National Honor Society induction ceremony. Missed it—and had no idea what to do. Should I barge in and demand my certificate and pin? Should I wait? Or was it better to hide? My legs shook, then gave out. I sank to the floor, closed my eyes, and let the linoleum cool my sweaty palms.

Half an hour later, when the doors swung open, I was still slumped on the floor. Maya Milansky floated from the auditorium, gold pin glowing on her collar, certificate clutched in her hand. We hadn't been friends since ninth grade, so when she spun and said, "We missed you, Sadie," it wasn't sympathy I heard in her voice. It was something sweeter—and nastier—all wrapped up in Maya's fake red hair and the fake butterfly tattoo on her ankle.

Other students filed out, followed by parents and teachers, each set giving me odd looks. The AP World History teacher, Mrs. Harmon, opened her mouth as if to say something consoling, but closed it and hurried off.

At least none of the parents or grandparents belonged to me. If there was a bright spot to this night, it was that. My mom died when I was three. All my memories of her were misty things. My grandmother wasn't well enough to attend—just a bad cold. Not that it stopped me from worrying. As for my dad? Well, the commute from Afghanistan was a long one.

I decided to search out the NHS advisor, get my pin and certificate, and make up a story about the ceremony for my grandmother.

Before I could stand, a shadow fell across my legs. Gordon Bakersfield stood so the toes of his shoes touched the heels of mine. In his hand, he held two certificates. He didn't smile, or give me any sort of look born of sympathy. He simply stared; the intensity in his eyes unnerved me.

I sighed. "I don't have time for this."

"You're right," he said. "You don't."

———

WHEN I LEFT school that night, the hands on the clock read 8:15. I had no memory of the lobby clearing, or parents leaving, or Gordon Bakersfield vanishing from my sight. All I remembered was sitting on the floor, linoleum chilling my legs, the National Honor Society certificate and pin by my side. Had Gordon done that?

Honestly, I didn't care. All I wanted was to keep my 4.0 GPA intact and ace the SAT. No problem. Until recently.

The next day, I stood at my locker, fingertips resting on the upper shelf, my gaze fixed on the dark inside. What had I wanted? To go to the library. Yes. But why?

Someone brushed my shoulder as the bell rang—someone with spiky black hair, dark eyes, and an intense stare. A burst of something flowed through my body. I could breathe again. My mind cleared. Of course! I was going to spend lunch at the library and finish an extra credit report.

Except. Gordon stood there, arms folded across his chest like he was guarding the way down the hall.

"Excuse me?" I said.

He stepped to one side. I grabbed a notebook and—before he could block the way again—raced up to the library.

In the library, Maya Milansky was working on what was no doubt the same extra credit report for AP World History. I sat down three tables away. She glanced up from her paper long enough to throw me a sneer. I threw one back. It never reached its target. Gordon slid into the chair opposite mine and caught the full force of my snark.

At least he blocked my view of Maya. Still. Back in ninth grade, I'd crushed hard on Gordon—one of those epic and deeply humiliating crushes. The kind that made you stalk his class schedule, so you could be at his locker when he was. The kind that had you biking past his house —multiple times. The kind where you confessed your entire heart to your best friend just to relieve a little of the pressure.

That best friend might have been Maya Milansky. Gordon might have gone to the freshman dance with her. From then on out, I'd pretended that neither existed.

Now I had no choice but to acknowledge at least one of them.

"What are you doing?" I asked.

Gordon shrugged. "Running interference."

World History was calling, so I said, "I don't have time for this." Whatever *this* was.

"You're right," he replied, in an echo from last night. "You don't."

I stared at him.

"Where do you think she—" He swiveled in his chair, pointing at Maya. Her hair fell forward, hiding her face in a curtain of red. "—gets all the time?"

Now it was my turn to shrug. Maya did everything I did—and then some—and managed to show up on time, too.

He leaned forward, eyes fixed on mine. "You."

I felt that burst again, my mind clearing, my thoughts all at once my own. My hand reached for my notebook, but Gordon's gaze transfixed me. My cheeks didn't heat up. I wasn't tongue-tied. But I couldn't glance away, either.

"Did you ever wonder where some people find the

time and energy to do everything while everyone else desperately tries to keep up?" he asked.

I nodded, slowly. For months now, the threads of my life had been hanging just out of my reach. No matter how hard I worked, I couldn't capture them and weave them back together.

"You know that saying, 'time is money'?" he continued.

"Yeah."

"And you know it's possible to steal money, right?"

"So?" I wasn't exactly sure where Gordon's train of thought was going, but I suspected the first stop was crazy-town.

"If it's possible to steal money. . . and time is money. . . come on, you're on the honor roll. Do the math."

*Right.* Crazy-town. Either that, or this was some elaborate practical joke that Maya had cooked up. I pushed back my chair.

"Really? You're doing this? After last night?" So I missed the ceremony. Why rub it in? I clutched my notebook tight to my chest in a feeble attempt to stop the ache. "I used to think you were a better person than that."

I left the library without looking back.

———

"SADIE! WAIT UP!"

Gordon's voice chased me down the hall. My head felt heavy on my neck. My stomach growled. I could pick up something at the snack bar. An apple, maybe. Something to restore my blood sugar and stop the persistent throb in my temples. Except I wasn't really hungry—not after the library.

"Sadie, please!"

Maybe it was that *please*, or the tone of his voice. I didn't turn around, but I slowed down. When Gordon landed next to me, panting, I realized I'd stopped right in front of his locker.

A flush burned my cheeks.

"Hear me out." Gordon raised a hand, as if that alone could hold me in place. "Then I won't bug you anymore."

I nodded, too stunned to protest.

"I know it sounds crazy, but it's possible to steal someone else's time." He gave me that intense stare again. His eyes, I realized, weren't just dark. They were the color of wet tree bark, but flecked with green. No matter how hard I'd tried during ninth grade, I'd never stood this close to Gordon before. The unfairness of that almost made me walk away.

"People steal time," I said, instead. "Right."

"Think about writer's block. It's the perfect example. Know where it comes from?"

I gave my head a little shake. As much as I hated to admit it, writing essays was getting harder and harder. I'd taken to waking up spontaneously at three a.m., my head filled with words, and writing then. But that was the only time I could.

"Ever sit down to write something but get nothing but a blank?" he asked.

He'd just described my school day, nothing but a great big white space.

"And even though you're there, and you think you're

working," he continued, "it feels like nothing. Or at least, that's how I think it feels."

"Don't you know how it feels?"

He shook his head. "No one's ever stolen my time."

Wow. This was insane. Gordon Bakersfield, of the epic ninth-grade crush, was insane. "You know what I think?" I said.

He leaned forward, ever so slightly, like he was certain of the outcome. I almost hated to disappoint him.

"I think you're wasting my time."

After two years of confusion and hurt, being the one to walk away was epic.

———

FOR THE REST of the week, I avoided Gordon. Or maybe he avoided me. The only person I couldn't lose was Maya. Library at lunch? There she was, two tables away. On the bleachers during open gym? Directly across from me, a perpetual smirk just visible in the parting of her red curtain hair.

And today, in the cafeteria? She stood up and moved closer to me.

*Closer*.

Fortunately, I'd finished my extra credit report early that morning—in another weird three a.m. writing session. First, I'd checked all the doors, even though I knew they were locked. With Dad gone, it was like the air had changed; it was thinner, harder to breathe, the house not just empty, but lonely.

I was examining some applesauce on my spoon (how

long I'd been holding it there was hard to say, but long enough to be embarrassing) when Gordon slid into the chair opposite mine.

"Look, I know you think I'm crazy, but she is seriously killing you." He whirled and nailed Maya with a look that made her head jerk back. If it weren't for the whole crazy factor, I might have clapped—just a little.

"No," I said, "she's just creeping me out. I can't get away from her."

"Because she's using you. She's sucking up all your time."

I spared Gordon a glance before contemplating my applesauce again. "Right."

"Think about it. What about the violin solo that should've been yours?"

His words knocked the appetite from me. I dropped the spoon. During auditions, my bow had come to a screeching halt. My violin hadn't screamed like that since sixth grade. It was like I'd murdered it, and I certainly butchered the audition.

"Where was Maya?" Gordon asked.

"Outside the . . ." I trailed off, not wanting to confess she'd been right outside the door when I left the audition.

"What happened today when she switched tables?"

My gaze darted toward my applesauce.

"Yeah. I'm sure it's fascinating stuff." He snorted. "But it took you five minutes to eat a single bite. And you know what she did during that time?" He jerked a thumb toward Maya.

I shook my head.

"Finished her extra-credit report. When did you do yours?"

"This morning." I raised my chin, but dropped it a second later, realizing the move highlighted the dark circles under my eyes. "At about three a.m."

"That's probably the only time you could." Gordon stood, hands planted on the cafeteria table. "Think about it this weekend when you're far away from her. Think about how you feel, about whether there's any difference. Then decide whether or not I'm crazy."

With that, Gordon walked away. I glanced toward Maya, bracing myself for that triumphant little smirk. Instead, she stared after Gordon, her red hair limp, eyes wide with a look I'd seen in my own.

It was terror.

———

I WOULD NEVER SAY I lived for the weekends. It was such a cliché.

But more and more it became my mantra. Not just because Dad was deployed and we got to Skype with him some weekends. (It was hit-or-miss, but he always tried.) All semester long, I'd chalked up the brain fog to Dad's deployment, to the too-quiet house at night, to how I'd wake at three a.m. and check all the locks before sitting down to finish my homework.

Now, I was contemplating a serious stop at crazy-town. Could Gordon be right? Could Maya actually steal time? For that matter, could anyone?

Saturday morning, I pulled the car keys from the hook

by the door. Grandma was in the yard, weeding, her face shaded by a huge straw hat, its brim covered in plastic apples. Back in middle school, I'd cringed every time she wore it in public. Today, the fact that she'd pulled it out and placed it on her head meant she'd shaken the cold. I couldn't help but smile.

The sun touched my face and made me squint. I shielded my eyes with a hand. "I think I'll study at the park today," I told her.

"A lovely idea, but don't stay too long. Your father might call."

"I know."

I headed for Five Mile Creek State Park, where Dad and I used to go camping. In a way, it was like being with him, only lonelier. Once there, I tried to think. That didn't sound like much, but I hadn't thought in ages. Not really. Now, with my chin propped on my knees, I allowed my thoughts to wander—daydreams of seeing Dad again and acing the SAT.

Stress, I decided, after a few hours. That was all. No one was stealing my time. I could forget all about Gordon and his crazy ideas.

Monday morning, five minutes after I walked into school, I lost everything—my willpower, my thoughts, my dreams. It was like a physical pull. I knew I had class and I knew I had to get there. But that's all I knew.

When I finally stumbled into first period World History and saw Maya Milansky fanning herself with an extra credit report—the 100% clearly visible—then glanced down at my measly 92%, something snapped.

I was going to find Gordon. I'd listen to what he had to

say. I'd do anything I could to get my time back, even if it meant booking a stay in crazy-town.

———

WE'D DEBATED where to meet. I didn't want to explain Gordon to Grandma. His house was in the same subdivision as Maya's, so that was out. We ended up in a strip mall coffee shop, a place called Jumpin' Java. It had tables in the back, away from the windows, which was where we sat.

"So," he prompted, "was I right?"

I hated to admit it, so I pulled my coffee toward me, but didn't drink.

He tipped back in his chair and took a sip of his Americano, clearly prepared to wait me out.

I sighed. "On Saturday, I drove out to the state park— no one around for miles." I waved my hands as if that could indicate a lack of people. "And I could . . . think again. I only spent two hours there, but I remember every single minute." Now, I leaned across the table, nudging my coffee cup out of the way. "Not only that, I remember living for each of those minutes. It was like going from bread and water to a buffet with an endless dessert bar."

Gordon's gaze fell to his Americano. I thought he wasn't going to say anything, and my strange confession had coffee-flavored bile burning the back of my throat.

"So. Yeah," he said at last. "Some people can steal time."

"Like Maya."

"Exactly like Maya."

"Like you?" It was a guess, an educated one, but still.

"Remember Title 1 in first grade?" he asked.

Amazingly, I did. It was one of those memories I'd pulled out during ninth grade and reexamined. The two of us were a team, sitting shoulder-to-shoulder, wrestling with the words on the page. The words confused me so much that the Title 1 teacher thought I must be dyslexic or have ADD.

"I didn't know it then," Gordon said, "but I was stealing your time to get through class."

"You what?"

He held up a hand. "I was six years old. All I knew was whenever I leaned against you, I could think better and make it through class."

"The teacher thought I was ADD."

He dropped his gaze, then peered up at me through thick black lashes. It was a swoon-worthy look. Part of me suspected he knew that. If he had done that during the epic ninth-grade crush, I might have fainted.

"Sorry?" He gave me a little shrug.

And that would've slain me. But I wasn't back in ninth grade; I was thinking about first. Over the summer, Grandma, disgusted with the teacher, had taken me to the library every day. She wrote articles that eventually found homes in places like *Ladies' Home Journal* and *Woman's Day*. I read. By September, I was reading at a fourth-grade level. Goodbye Title 1 and hello challenge reading.

"Do you steal time now?" I asked.

"Look," he said, like I'd bumped a recent bruise. "People are incredibly careless with their time." He cocked his head, his expression thoughtful. "Imagine if everyone let dollar bills float out of their pockets and litter the street. Would you blame me for walking behind them and picking up all that cash?"

"Technically, isn't that stealing?"

"If the other person doesn't miss it, does it matter?"

"I'm seriously missing my time," I said.

"That's because you have quality time."

"What?"

"You're smart and creative." Gordon's cheeks went this amazing pink. It made his dark eyes brighten so I could see the tiny flecks of green. Deep down, the embers of that long-ago crush flared. My own cheeks heated. Between us, we could've brewed a fresh pot of coffee.

"You really don't want some people's time," he continued, "like if they're drunk or high. Easy to steal, but pretty worthless."

"Oh."

"And some adults, like workaholics?" Gordon rolled his eyes. "Just clutter and full of static."

"Can anyone steal time?"

"I don't know. Some people seem born to it."

"Like you?"

"Maybe."

"What about Maya?"

"Maya's special. She's a time leech."

"A what?"

"You know that saying about how everyone has the same twenty-four hours in a day?"

I nodded.

"Well, if you can figure out how to steal time, you end up with more—or at least better—time. Maya's been using yours. It's why I've been trying to run interference. That's why I gave you a little bit of my time."

"You can do that?"

"It was extra, from someone else, and I didn't really need it."

Those little bursts. I felt my eyes grow wide. Despite everything, I smiled. "That was you?"

He nodded. "Except, I can't always do that. I mean, I won't always be around."

"How do I get rid of her?"

"I don't know."

"Can I learn to steal time?"

"No idea."

Then what was the point to all this? "So you're trying to help me, but have no idea how to do that?"

"Pretty much."

I sighed, took a sip of my coffee, but it had gone cold. I scrunched up my nose and Gordon laughed. "I'll buy you another," he said.

"And then what?"

He stood, picked up my cup, and gave me a grin. "Time will tell."

———

ACCORDING TO GORDON, you didn't actually need to touch people to steal their time, not when you got good at it. But you did need proximity. In my case, distance was the best defense. I could simply avoid Maya when he wasn't around.

And when he was, like in AP World History, Maya

faded into the background. Gordon talked Mrs. Harmon into letting him switch seats, so he sat by me and, as he called it, ran interference. Maya scowled, but I hardly cared. At last, I could breathe in that room, and concentrate on the lecture, and earn 100% on extra credit reports.

We returned to Jumpin' Java, day after day. Gordon schooled me in the finer points of time thievery; I asked endless questions.

"How did you figure it out?" I asked him during one of our sessions.

"Over time," he said, then grinned as if he'd been waiting forever to tell time jokes. "Seriously, you get a feel for it. You start recognizing who else can do it too."

"Any honor among thieves?"

"Not really."

"Is that why you're helping me?"

He grinned again. "Maybe."

Unfortunately, when it came to technique, my mind couldn't grasp even the basics. Intellectually, this new interpretation of time fascinated me. On a practical level? It was Title 1 all over again. More often than not, I drifted off, savoring the luxury of un-stolen time. Gordon was the salt for my time leech.

Not that he was always happy about that.

"You're daydreaming," he said during another session at the coffee shop.

"I am?"

"I can feel it."

"You can?"

"Yeah. So cut it out."

I hadn't daydreamed in ages, it seemed, and I hated to give it up just because he said so. I touched my cheek as if that could bring back the elusive images floating just out of reach. They had been, in fact, images about Gordon—

"I said, cut it out." He pulled my hand from my cheek and gripped my fingers. "It's like a beacon, okay? I'm surprised every time thief in a five-mile radius hasn't come crashing in here. I'm surprised Maya hasn't—"

The bell over the door jangled and in waltzed Maya, violin case swinging from one hand, book bag slung over the other shoulder.

"Time to leave," Gordon said.

"What?" I glanced at my half-full cup of coffee, then to his face, his eyes dark and fierce. I blinked a few times, trying to collect all my stray thoughts. We'd been doing . . . what?

"Wow. That was fast." He stepped to the side, blocking Maya's line of sight. All at once, my thoughts were mine again.

"Come on." Gordon extended a hand to help me up. "Let's leave before you end up needing a time transfusion."

I hated being so helpless—the classic damsel in distress. I hated those, too. There had to be a way I could fight Maya on my own, so she'd leave me alone, once and for all.

In orchestra, we sat side by side, her first chair to my second. Mentally, I tried pushing her away. Her grin told me I was like a toddler trying to wrestle with a ten-year-old—cute and totally ineffective.

The only relief came when Maya played her solo, the

highlight of our upcoming spring concert. For weeks, I lived for that moment. For weeks, I never knew why. Then, that Friday, it hit me. When she was the only one playing, she couldn't steal time. Her full concentration was on that solo, and every last bit of my leeched time came rushing back. It made me wonder.

What if I tried to steal Maya's time?

I focused all my attention on her, bit my lower lip in concentration. I thought about Gordon giving me some of his extra time, how it felt like a burst—a cool drink of water on a hot day. Maybe time wasn't like money at all. Maybe it was more fluid, more like water. You could bend it and make it do what you wanted it to, if only you knew how.

So I imagined sucking up Maya's time through a straw. All at once, I felt that little burst. Not as intense as when Gordon had given me time, but still there, still wonderful.

Maya's violin screamed.

―――――

MAYA CAME after me in the hall outside of Orchestra. She shoved me into a practice room, her arms like steel from years on the violin. She slammed the door behind us, then leaned against it so I couldn't escape. We were both going to be late for next block. When I opened my mouth to speak, no words came out.

"That wasn't funny," she said.

"Yeah. Well, now you know how I feel."

"You don't have a clue."

In a way, Maya and I were alike, both of us girls whose

names kids remembered during calculus and then forgot by lunch. We filled our days overachieving—extra credit reports, extracurriculars, extra-everything—to forget how lonely we were. And once upon a time, we'd been friends.

"I don't know what I did to you," I said, "but—"

"Right. Like you and Gordon aren't laughing about it."

"Laughing about what?" Nothing about this was funny: not Maya stealing my time, and not me stealing hers.

She pushed off the door and stepped close enough that I could see where the red in her hair ended and the brown roots began.

"Here's what you don't understand," she said. "It's an addiction. And there's no rehab for it, no twelve-step program. And do you know just how dangerous it is to get between an addict and his supply?"

Was she threatening me? Really? After all this? This time, I stepped closer. "I just messed up your solo," I told her. "I can do it again." At least, I was pretty sure I could.

Her lip curled in a sneer. "I've been doing this for years, and you're way behind the learning curve."

The bell for last block rang, then a hush fell over the hallway. I was a statue in the center of the room. Maya's hand was frozen on the doorknob.

"Listen," she said, and if her voice wasn't softer, at least it wasn't harsh. "You're the one who needs to be scared, okay? Just don't say I didn't warn you."

With that, she threw open the door and ran from the room.

―――

"WHAT DID I ever do to Maya?"

The question had been haunting me since yesterday. Gordon and I sat, not in the coffee shop, but in that quiet corner of Five Mile Creek. Spring had cast a soft green over everything and brought out the flecks in Gordon's eyes. I was resisting the urge to get lost in their depths, but it was a battle I didn't mind losing. Earlier, I'd told him about how I'd stopped Maya's solo and he'd given me a high five.

Now he plucked at the grass that poked up around the blanket we sat on. "I don't know. Maybe it's because I had a crush on you in ninth grade?"

My head shot up. My heart pounded so hard, I thought it might pop through not only my ribs but the skin surrounding my chest.

"No," I said. "You didn't. You went to the freshman dance with Maya."

"Only because she told me that you thought I was a total creeper."

"She told you that?"

He gave his head an emphatic nod.

"But—" My mouth hung open, but I lacked the willpower to shut it, so stunned was I by this revision of history. "I liked you."

My words came out soft, so soft, I almost hoped the breeze would catch them and steal them away. But Gordon jerked his head, almost like I'd slapped him. His Adam's apple bobbed.

"You . . . liked . . . me." Each word he spoke grew slower, so I wasn't sure if he'd finished talking or not.

"You never wondered why I was always at your locker?" I shook my head, both in disbelief and to rid my cheeks of the shame that heated them. "Or why I rode my bike past your house a hundred times every weekend?"

"I just thought I was lucky."

He kissed me then, one hand on the back of my head, my mouth still open and gaping, so it was just his lips and a lot of air. I exhaled. He inhaled. For one instant, we shared the same breath.

"Do you steal everything?" I said at last.

"Nothing that can get me arrested."

He kissed me again. This time, he didn't have to steal anything at all.

———

MONDAY MORNING AT SCHOOL, one glance at Gordon sent my insides twisting. No green glowed in his eyes. His skin was dull. Not a trace remained of the sunny, happy boy I'd spent Saturday with.

"We need to talk," he said.

Every last hope sank to the pit of my stomach. I'd spent Sunday in blissful daydreams—walking the halls with Gordon, hand in hand, eating lunch with him every day, side by side. I'd even let my mind stray to next year— the homecoming dance, prom. Now, crashing through all that? A talk we needed to have.

"When?" I said, mainly because it was the only word I could force from my throat.

"After school."

The bell rang. Gordon vanished. Students pushed past me on the way to homeroom. I stood there, dumb and numb. In those moments, no one stole my time. I doubt they could have. Every ounce of feeling I had was channeled into Gordon. I didn't have any time to spare, even for myself, and I barely made it to homeroom before the second bell echoed through the empty halls.

If Maya stole any of my time that day, I didn't notice. I suspect it really wasn't worth stealing. Who wanted time that was sad, anxious, and depressed? Because I already knew how the conversation would go. Gordon would play nervously with his Americano. He'd tell me how great I was, but ninth grade was a long time ago, and while he liked me, he didn't *like* like me.

Blah, blah, blah.

For once, I wished Maya would steal my time, if only so I wouldn't have to notice the ache of each passing minute. In AP World History, Gordon slipped me a note. All it said was:

*Coffee shop*

I walked there alone. I ordered alone. I sat alone, for five minutes, until Gordon flew through the door like he'd sprinted the entire distance between the school and his afternoon Americano. He rushed past the counter without ordering.

Hard and quick then, with no small talk, no *you're great, but . . .*

"I'm sorry," he said, his words insubstantial from lack of air.

"I know. I get it. You don't want to see me anymore."

"What? No. I want to see you every day. I want to spend every moment I can with you."

Mere seconds ticked by, but I savored each one, simply

so I could savor those words. Whatever came next would make my heart ache.

"Then . . . why?" I said when he didn't speak.

"You don't need me anymore. The fact you can mess up Maya's solo gives you enough power to make it through the rest of the school year. Next fall, you'll figure out something else to keep her in check."

"But that doesn't have anything to do with . . ." The word stuck in my mouth.

"Us?" Gordon said, as if he'd plucked the word from my tongue. "Well, that's just it. Keeping Maya in check is one thing. Keeping me in check?" He shook his head. "Not going to happen."

"Why would I need to do that? You've been—"

"Helping you? Is that what you think?"

"Well, yeah."

He laughed, but it wasn't the happy sound from Saturday. "Remember when I explained how Maya was a time leech?"

The coffee in my stomach iced over. I nodded.

"How do you think I knew that? Why do you think I even cared what Maya did?"

"Because—" I began, but Gordon wouldn't let me finish.

"She was poaching on my territory."

"Your territory?" I didn't like the sound of that.

"You," he said.

I was right. I didn't like it.

"I've been stealing time from you since first grade. Back then, all I knew was sitting next to you made me feel better—smarter. When you were close by, I could read the book or finish all the math problems. I've been doing it for so long, I don't know how to live in real time anymore."

Maya's angry words slammed into me and I understood what she'd meant that day in the practice room. "You're addicted."

"To stealing time?" Gordon snorted. "Yeah, maybe. You could call it that."

"What were you going to do?" I demanded. "Follow me to college? Live next door?"

"Marry you?"

All of this, just for some time. Was the story about his crush fake? Were those kisses in the state park all fake too? Tears burned my eyes and a deep shame made my fingers tremble against the coffee cup. I couldn't pick it up, but I couldn't let go of it either.

"I like you too much to keep stealing your time. But if I'm going to stop, I can't be near you. It just isn't possible. Even now, during all this." He reached forward and caught a tear with his thumb before I could jerk away from his touch. "Even now, I've been stealing bits of time."

Even now? My mouth fell open and my tears dried on their own.

"Think of money again," he said. "It's like you're standing in the middle of the road and tossing endless twenty-dollar bills into the air for anyone to take."

"Oh. So this is all my fault."

"I used to think that. I used to think that it didn't matter if I took a little of your time, since you had so much and were so generous." He shrugged. "But it hurts you. It's wrong. And if I can't be with you, at least I know I'm not hurting you."

Gordon stood. He held himself stiff, like a soldier on a parade ground, and left the coffee shop by the back entrance. When the screen door bounced shut, I sank into my chair, my limbs useless, my coffee cold and congealed with cream.

My heart, smashed.

The coffee shop's front door swung open. The bell clanged and I winced. It was as if Gordon's confession had made every inch of me extra sensitive. I glanced up, half hoping Gordon had returned, half hoping this was some sort of cruel practical joke and—with time—I'd forgive him, half hoping I'd only imagined the last fifteen minutes.

Instead, Maya strode into the coffee shop.

———

I SAW the moment she registered that it was just me at the table. Her eyes went wide. Her steps slowed, but not so anyone else noticed. She looked almost disappointed. Then that familiar smirk spread across her face.

I slid my foot around the leg of the chair opposite me, so when Maya pulled, it didn't go anywhere. She yanked and the wood scarred my ankle.

"Where's the addict?" she said, her voice all syrupy sweet. "It's not like him to leave his supply unguarded."

"Sorry, but the time store is closed—to him, and to you."

"Hardly. You have no idea what you're doing."

"Actually, I have no idea what *you're* doing. Maya, we used to be friends. What happened?"

"He did. You did. You got everything you wanted. Your dad totally spoiled you. Your grandmother never bitched about your GPA, and the cutest boy in our grade had a ginormous crush on you. What's not to hate?"

Her words didn't feel as harsh as they sounded. And all that hatred? Never touched me. It was all turned in on herself.

"Of course, then I figured out why he liked you." She blew a bubble with the gum she was chewing and, when it popped, added, "I guess it's better than him liking you just for your tits, you know?"

"When did you become such a cynic?"

"Ninth grade."

It was true, of course, that Dad did spoil me. Only child of a single parent? It happened. The moment he walked in from his deployment, he'd want to take me to Build-a-Bear and the amusement park. And I was going to let him. It was as if every time he went away, he forgot how old I was. I didn't just freeze in time; I went backward. And if Maya couldn't remember a thing about me from all those years ago, then this wasn't a relationship I could salvage.

I stood and planted my palms on the table. The surface was clammy, my skin hot and slick. I held fast and leaned forward.

"Let's get one thing straight," I said to her. "Steal any more of my time and I will ruin you."

"I'd like to see you try."

"Think you'll make concertmaster next year if you botch the solo at the spring concert?"

Maya's jaws went still.

"You know I can do it." Maybe it was the only thing I could do, but Gordon was right. It was all I needed to keep her in check. "Remember that every time you pick up your bow."

I pushed away from the table, making it rock. My half-empty cup toppled over. I grabbed my book bag, slung it over my shoulder, and left the coffee shop.

I was never coming back.

———

FOR THE FIRST time in ages (possibly since first grade), I had time to myself. I'd glance at the clock after finishing my homework to find the evening stretching long and leisurely before me. The late-day sun filled our back porch, making the whitewash glow. I took to playing my violin there—Maya's solo piece in particular—just to prove I could.

"I simply can't imagine why you didn't get the solo," Grandma said one night. "That other girl must be something else."

"Yeah," I said, holding the length of the violin against me. "She is."

If you ever wanted to bottle up awkwardness and shame, all you needed to do was walk into first-block AP World History. Gordon had switched seats again. Maya never looked my way. The air was thick with static from broken hearts and broken dreams and broken hopes over the final exam.

Anyone with a passing acquaintance with Mrs.

Harmon's grading structure knew the final counted for fifty percent of the grade.

"Relax, people. It's not the end of the world," she said the day of the exam. "You still have time to raise your grade. If anyone wants to know the ins and outs of an extra credit report, talk to Sadie or Maya."

Maya would probably tell them how to do it backwards, not that anyone would ask her—or me, for that matter. The thought struck hard, another blow against my smashed heart. No one would ask me. That was more than shameful. It was downright sad.

The AP World History final was the easiest test I have ever taken in my entire life. I knew all the answers—almost before I finished reading the questions. I went over the test twice. The idea of walking to the front of the room and plopping the year's hardest exam onto Mrs. Harmon's desk, after only twenty minutes, seemed insane.

What was I going to do with all this time? Or maybe I could steal a little more. What then? Perfect scores on the SAT? *New Yorker*–ready college application essays? Valedictorian? It was all there, all within my grasp. Wasn't that what Maya was doing? I glanced toward her, a burst of something sweet and rancid filling me. *Schadenfreude*. A word I'd learned last year in German. Joy at the misfortune of others.

I never wanted to feel that again.

Exam paper in hand, I stood. A few students murmured behind me, a muted "No way!" summing up the room's general opinion. Mrs. Harmon raised an eyebrow, both skeptical and a little impressed.

I halted halfway to her desk. Maya looked grim, her

pencil logging answers like a marathoner who had hit the wall—slow, deliberate tracks across her paper. A sheen of sweat covered Gordon's forehead. He was maybe a third of the way through the exam. And I knew this: he wouldn't finish.

You could hoard time, hold it tight and miserly against your chest. You could steal it from others, leaving them gasping and grasping. But could you give it away?

I thought about what Gordon had said, about how it was like I was standing in the middle of the road, throwing twenty-dollar bills into the air for all to take. I remembered how I felt when Gordon gave me a bit of his time—how that was even better than taking it from Maya.

So I stood in the middle of AP World History and thought about how fluid time was. Instead of sucking it all in with a giant straw, I imagined a fountain, filled with endless water, its spray covering everything. Just enough water to cool Maya's hand and wash the sweat from Gordon's face.

Eyes closed, I brought my fingertips to my lips and blew the gentlest of kisses. Like dropping a pebble into still water, the ripples flowed, touching each student in the classroom. Something shifted behind me. Pens scratched faster against paper. I didn't turn to look. Instead, I accepted the library pass Mrs. Harmon offered and took the steps to the third floor slowly, savoring each one.

I'm pretty sure I daydreamed.

———

I STILL DON'T KNOW what happened that day, but the effects continued to ripple throughout the entire school. Everyone passed the AP World History exam. Our combined average SAT and ACT scores were the highest in the state. The hallways felt different. Kids smiled and said hello. I did help a few classmates with AP World History extra credit reports. The girls from my calculus class invited me to eat lunch with them. They even remembered my name.

I had a sense for time now, too, like I could feel it flowing around me, through me, and through the school itself. If someone was sucking down too much of it, I'd reverse the flow—or give the hapless victim some of my own time. I'd learned to exist on a shoestring budget. I almost didn't know what to do with the surplus I had now.

It was the last week of school when Gordon Bakersfield spoke to me again. I was on my way home, soaking up the June sun, when he ran up behind me. The footfalls had me turning around before my mind realized this wasn't a boy who deserved any of my time.

"Look, I know what you're going to say." He held both hands outstretched, like I was a skittish deer who'd bolt at any second. "Hear me out?"

"I think I've given you enough of my time," I said. "Besides, my dad will be home from Afghanistan in less than a month." I fell quiet. Time might be fluid, but it could still feel static—if hopeful. *Less than a month.*

"I'm spending all my time with him," I added.

"That's great," he said. "I'm glad for you guys."

He sounded that way, too. Glad. Sincere. Honest. My

stomach clenched. I knew better than to trust him. If Gordon were an alcoholic, I'd be a walking bottle of Jack Daniel's.

"But here's the thing," he said. "I'm trying hard to live in real time."

"I know." My cheeks grew warm, and I hoped he'd think that was just the sun. "I mean, I can tell. At school, at least."

"You can tell when someone steals time?"

I nodded.

"And you can—" He mimicked juggling. "—change things up, like that day in World History?"

Again, I nodded.

"You're like the sheriff of time."

"More like Robin Hood," I said. "I'm just leveling the playing field."

Gordon laughed. "So I'm trying. And it's hard. I could use the help. Plus—" He broke off, shook his head. "Naw, it's silly. You wouldn't be interested."

"In what?'

"I want to learn how to daydream and I thought you could teach me how."

"You can't teach someone to daydream."

"How would you know? Have you tried?"

"You just can't, that's all."

"Wow. I never pegged you for a cynic."

If Gordon Bakersfield had used any other word that day, I would've walked away.

"I'll need proof you're sincere," I said.

"I know that."

"As in every-single-day proof you're sincere."

"That's a given."

"And I'm not going to trust you for a long time, maybe never."

"Oh, you'll trust me eventually."

"You think so?" I tried for stern, but I noticed we'd fallen into step and those steps were leading us to the coffee shop.

"Sure," Gordon said. "It's just a matter of time."

## What Little Remains

IN THE MORNINGS, I slip out the broken window so anyone still living in this building will not hear me. Footfalls echo in the empty hallway, and since debris blocks the stairwell to the roof, no one climbs to the top anymore.

Except me. But I take the long way.

I slide along the tenth-floor ledge, rough bricks scraping my shoulder blades, heels locked against the building. My fingertips inch from brick face to mortar. It's this I concentrate on. To think of the fall is to wish for it.

In the mornings, mist hides the city and dampens the stench of rotted wood and flesh. In the mornings, I inhale the scent of damp soil from the rooftop garden and the sharp odor from the volunteer tomato plants. When I was little, I always imagined the plants with tiny flintlock rifles over their shoulders, marching from one garden to the next. I know better now. But as I tug weeds from around their stems, I like to think we're both fighting a good fight.

This morning, when I pull myself onto the rooftop, my foot strikes a rake. The handle flips up and plops back onto the tarpaper shingles. I freeze, certain that yesterday I left the rake leaning against the stairwell to the floors below. I take a cautious look around.

In the garden itself, a set of footprints, much larger than my own, crosses the expanse. Tiny hairs prickle on the back of my neck, like someone has come from behind and blown a stream of air against my skin. I remain stricken.

By the time the sun touches my face, my feet ache, and my calf muscles knot, so when I do move, my gait is hobbled. I study the outline of the footprints. Some sort of heavy work boot—the depression is deep and the soil crushed. Yet my spindly volunteer tomatoes stand proud, all green except for a faint yellow blush. No one has tugged on a carrot or dug a potato. The soil is moist. The watering can sits on the east side of the garden, not the west, where I left it yesterday. And then, of course, there's the matter of the displaced rake.

Only when the sun warms the top of my head do I notice them. My heart jolts. I grip the rake, certain I'll snap the ancient wood in half. There, on the roof's edge, is a perfect set of fingernails—the press-on kind, that, once upon a time, were advertised on TV. They are such a brilliant red, they make the brickwork around them look dull and dowdy. They are so pristine and lined up so exactly, I'm surprised they're not attached to some starlet hanging on for dear life, waiting for the man in those heavy work boots to clomp across my garden and rescue her.

I whirl around, certain he's here to do just that. The roof is empty. A breeze rustles the leaves of the tomato plants. They bow their heavy heads and whisper to each other. They will not tell me what they know.

———

ALL WEEK, I sneak up to the garden earlier and earlier, until there's a danger I'll miss the ledge in the dark. Fresh footprints greet me each morning. Mid-week, someone clears the scum from the top of the water in the rain barrel. Weeds gather in wilted piles along the edges of the garden's cedar container. Most unsettling, every day I find a set of press-on nails in the same spot. Today they glow sparkly pink, glitter catching the early morning light.

Something compels me to search for the starlet. I kneel at the ledge, stretch out a hand. It's silly, but at the same time, I'd want someone to reach out for me. Today, the sun strikes my face at the same moment my fingers reach the air beyond the ledge. A burst of light blinds me. Wind kicks up dust, and I duck my head.

Warm hands with sharp nails grip my arm. I jerk backward and tumble across the roof. Someone tumbles with me. After the noise and light, all is quiet except our haggard breaths.

"I'm through!" the girl next to me says. "And look! My fingernails. I thought I'd lost them for sure."

Her clothes flow with her every move. Her hair is tall, so tall, maybe taller than her head—well, at least the bangs are. Brilliant blue is smeared across her eyelids. Dark pink streaks her cheeks. And her lips are as red as my tomatoes should be. I touch my own face, but brick dust and mud can never compare.

"Are you an actress?" I ask.

"What?" She shakes her head, but her hair barely moves. "No, silly. I just live—" Her brow creases and she scans the rooftop. "Well, here, but not here." Her gaze travels until it reaches the garden. "Oh, how strange. I keep wondering how my grandmother's garden changes. But it doesn't. I'm just seeing yours."

"Thank you for pulling my weeds," I say.

She laughs. "But then I get in trouble for not pulling my grandmother's. And I always put my nails there." She points to the ledge. "So I won't ruin them. I thought the wind was blowing them away."

The air shimmers above the nails. Something bright flashes from the space beyond but vanishes before I can even grasp what it might be.

"I'm Shelli, by the way, with an i." She stands and her clothes flutter, their colors startling, like the blue jays and goldfinches you still sometimes see.

Her feet are tiny, her shoes so clean and bright. They do not have the heavy soles that crisscross my garden and trample the soil.

"I'm Kit," I say, "with an i."

Shelli laughs, but as she walks the rooftop's perimeter, her features grow somber. "This isn't all like my grandmother said it would be."

"She's been here?"

"A long time ago." Shelli shields her eyes with a hand and peers out over the ledge. "Is this the end of the world?"

"No, unfortunately."

She scrunches up her face. "The future, then?"

I shrug. That glimmer catches my eye again. I wonder what it is about my rooftop that makes the air do that. I wonder what it is about my rooftop that brings strangers to me.

"I'm from 1999," she says. "What year is it here?"

Some claim to know the year, but no two claims match. I've since stopped caring, so all I do is shake my head.

Shelli leans forward where the ledge is still waist high. "I go to school ..." She points. "There."

I follow her gaze and her finger to the charred remains, where wisps of smoke rise in the morning mist. "I used to go there," I say.

Her mouth turns down, but she is still so pretty. I want to work in her grandmother's garden, have shiny, tall hair, and fancy nails—a different color on each finger. I do not want to stay on my rooftop. I do not want to use everything I have to coax tomatoes from the soil. I want to go to a place where hope still lives.

"I don't know how to bring you back," she says, as if reading my mind. "I'm not even sure how I got through."

"That's okay." But the words leave my mouth with a sigh.

Her gaze darts from black-streaked buildings to my garden and then to me. "It's not really okay."

She's right, of course, but I don't have words to tell her that. "I want to show you something," I say instead and point to the heavy footprints in the garden. At the sight of them, it feels like a boot is crushing my heart. "Someone else is slipping through."

Shelli kneels at the garden's edge and traces the impression as if that will tell her what we need to know. She says, "Be careful." And I think that maybe it has.

Before I can respond, all the air around us is sucked away. I duck my head, bring a hand up to cover my nose and mouth. Soil and dust swirl around me. Grit stings my eyes. Then, all is quiet. Shelli is gone. Only her pink, sparkly nails remain, not clinging to the edge, but at my feet in a little pile. I scoop them up and hold one against my finger.

Oh, so pretty.

———

TODAY, I find the tomatoes crushed, their seeds and pulp spread across the garden, their juice soaking into the soil. I tunnel my fingers beneath the dirt, excavating tiny bits of green flesh in hopes of saving it. My efforts only drive the dirt deeper into what little remains.

I gather the tomatoes anyway. Perhaps with water from the rain barrel, I can rinse the bigger chunks clean—or clean enough. Perhaps ...

The slap of the rake handle against tarpaper shingles forces my gaze up. At first, all I see are big, white boots, with heels so enormous, they could smash my largest tomatoes with one step—and probably have. His clothes do not billow. They are sleek and stiff, an exoskeleton that encases him from foot to head. The man before me is not from the past, not like Shelli. If he's from the future, then I think humanity may be better off among the remains. My gaze darts to the building's edge and the nails there— a set of brilliant blue. Only today, one nail points toward the rooftop stairwell.

"You don't belong here," I say to the man.

His image flickers then solidifies again.

"This isn't your world."

More flickering, but he stubbornly stays on my rooftop. Not only that, but he takes a step forward, followed by another.

I dodge his steps, like a mouse out-maneuvering a feral cat. The toe of one boot catches me and sends me flying toward the building's edge. I roll, palms scraping tarpaper and grit. I grip the ledge, stop my descent, heart thudding against the brick, lungs inhaling dust. When I open my eyes, bright blue nails greet me, pointed toward the stairwell. I scramble to my feet and dash for safety.

Shelli flings open the door and pulls me inside. "Thank God! You're okay."

"You too."

We cling to each other in the shelter of the stairwell.

"He can't open the door," she says.

"Did he try?"

Shelli nods and I clutch her tighter.

"What do we do?" she asks.

I shake my head. What can we do? He's already destroyed my garden. Once the noon sun strikes the rooftop, cowering in the stairwell won't be an option. We'll broil in here, and with the stairs blocked, there's no way down. Perhaps the two of us could rush him, using our combined strength to push him over the ledge.

I open my mouth to voice this idea, but can't force the words from my throat. So little remains—of my garden, of this world—that I don't want to take one more life, even one that doesn't belong here.

In front of us, the man crouches, lifts a handful of tomato and soil to his face. He pushes back his visor and inhales as if it's the most wonderful thing he's ever smelled. Then, he turns toward us. Sorrow washes across his face. His mouth moves. After a long moment, I piece together his words.

*I'm sorry.*

Oh, and so am I.

"He's trapped," I say to Shelli. "He's not in this world, or his own, but in between."

She nods, but her eyes are huge, the beautiful blue around them caked and creased. Dark smears travel down her cheeks. I venture from the stairwell, Shelli gripping my hand.

"You need to get back," I say to the man. "Right?"

The sorrow fades, and he nods. He steps from the garden, trailing mud and tomato innards. I try not to cringe at the destruction or his approach.

"There must be a way." I glance toward the now-empty ledge. "Shelli! Your nails! They're gone."

I creep forward and take the man by one of his stiff, gloved hands. His fingers swallow mine whole. The safety of the stairwell is too far away; he is too strong. But he trots by my side like a compliant puppy.

"Where, exactly?" I ask Shelli.

She bends over, hair sweeping the bricks. "Here, where this dent is." She peers at me through the strands of hair. "My grandmother told me to stand here and wish upon a star. Funny how it's lasted all this time."

We position the man at the ledge and stand across from him. An urge hits me, like I should salute. Instead I stretch out my hand. A smile lights his face that makes him look like an action hero. He shakes my hand, then Shelli's.

Then, it's as if the wind steals him. When the dust settles, speckling my arms and face, nothing remains except for me, the crushed tomatoes, and one of Shelli's bright blue fingernails.

———

FOOTPRINTS no longer mar my garden. The rooftop's ledge looks lonely without Shelli's colorful nails. I may have salvaged a tomato plant. A week has passed, and it seems to have a hold on the soil, if a tenuous one. I am its fiercely protective mother. I spend hours on the roof, chasing away chattering crows, providing sips of water from the rain barrel.

This morning when I crest the rooftop, something bulky sits on the opposite ledge. I creep forward slowly, still on all fours. There, in the spot where Shelli's nails used to clutch the edge, a basket of tomatoes sits, along with packets of seeds. Beneath those, I uncover a set of press-on nails, the very shade of the tomatoes.

The sun hits the ledge, warming the tomatoes, making

their skin glow. The nails dazzle my eyes. Together, they are the color of blood and hope.

And oh, so pretty.

*What Little Remains* was first published in The Maze: Three Tales of the Future by Collins Mark Books, July 2014.

## The Maze

### Eppie

ON THE TWELFTH DAY, Cadet Eppie Langtry found the cracks in the wall.

She'd stopped her trek through the maze and leaned against its smooth surface. Exhaustion from the first six hours washed through her, the force of it pushing her into the unforgiving wall. After a few quick breaths, she wiped a hand across her eyes and rolled her shoulder. It was nothing more than a simple push to get going. But beneath her, something shifted.

Eppie sprang back, gulping cold air. She inched closer and probed the crevice with her fingers. The unrelenting and unchanging wall of the past twelve days slid against her skin. She nudged the wall with her shoulder, the way you might a best friend, as if she and this impenetrable white slab had anything in common. The crevice deepened.

Eppie glanced upward. The walls and ceiling were bare, but so bright that some days, she wanted to crouch into a ball, bury her head in her arms, and simply rock the twelve hour shift away.

She never did. The stories of those who had halted for too long kept her trudging forward through the maze. With her shoulder molding new shapes in the wall, Eppie latched onto the first glimmer of ... *something*. Like everyone else in her class, she'd spent hours pounding the surface, scratching the walls, kicking as hard as she could. Not even blood from torn fingernails was a match for the bright, white glare. Worse, after that first day, everyone's boots went missing from their lockers, and they now navigated the icy maze in bare feet.

Her toes ached with the cold. Eppie sandwiched one foot on top of the other and inspected the dip in the wall her shoulder had made. She poked at the wall with her fingertips, and the pliant give became unrelenting again. It was as if the maze resented her earlier attempts of kicking and scratching.

Eppie blew out a breath. "I'd be resentful too," she said, her words barely reaching her ears. It was as if the walls absorbed both the sound of her voice and what she had to say.

She tried her shoulder again, rolling it around, gentle, persistent, but giving it a bit of rhythm, like a dance routine. If the cadre were filming this—and no doubt they were—she must look ridiculous. A giggle escaped her lips, and Eppie slapped a hand across her mouth. She hadn't laughed in how many days? Certainly not the last twelve.

Beneath her shoulder, the crevice grew into a valley. Since the wall seemed to like her shoulder, what about a hip? Now she *was* dancing. Hip, shoulder, step. Hip, shoulder, step. Hip, shoulder...

Something solid and warm blocked her progress. Eppie halted, drinking in the first hint of heat in more than six hours. Was this the key, then? Movement? Friction? The wall beneath her still glowed white. It looked deceptively cold, but its warmth was delicious. She turned her face toward the wall, tongue flicking across her lips. What if she leaned forward? What if she let her mouth graze the surface? What then?

She was a mere breath away when the wall beneath her skin coughed.

## Hank

Cadet Hank Su stomped through the corridor. No matter how hard he tried, the bright white swallowed the sound of his footfalls until all that remained were small, pathetic steps against the frigid floor. No matter how hard he screamed, the walls absorbed it. By dinner, his throat was so raw, even water scraped on the way down. He crashed from side to side. He kicked until they took away his boots. He gathered up all his strength and bolted down the corridor.

Gentle curves morphed into straight, hard surfaces— almost on a whim—and he slammed into the wall, this time not on purpose. Hank experimented with speed, sprints and slow jogs, but always moving forward. After that first day, when his best friend Ryan didn't come back, Hank had known this was no ordinary training exercise. Every night, he confronted that empty bunk next to his. To stop seeing the image of the stripped mattress and empty footlocker, Hank bent his head forward and ran with all his strength, grateful for the crash at the end.

But today, day twelve, he walked the corridors, keeping his pace steady. When he stood still, the walls closed in. If he extended his arms, certainly he'd be able to touch both sides at once. Every time he tried? The walls exhaled. There was no other word for it. And they left him standing in the center of the hall, fingertips straining for the cold surface on either side of him.

An illusion. A trick. Something someone was recording. Would the cadre play it back, at the end of the exercise, so everyone could laugh at him? He shook his head, banishing that notion—and the thought that there was no end to this. That was why they punched the walls. That was why they kicked. Didn't the cadre understand that? Or maybe they did, and that was the point.

Hank inched closer to one wall, letting his fingers trail along its surface. So smooth. So cold. An ache bloomed beneath his fingertips. He moved closer still, resting his forehead against the wall. The shock of cold almost made him jerk back. But as unrelenting as the wall was, it soothed his brow, made his throat feel less parched. Hank inhaled, held the recycled air in his lungs, then blew out a long breath and pitched forward.

There, on the wall—like the indentation on a pillow— was the impression of his forehead. With hands and fingers, he probed the dent. Nothing. In frustration, he leaned his head in the same spot, and the wall gave way again.

This time, Hank stood still. The corridor remained quiet. The lights blared down, like they always had. A dry, stale taste had invaded his mouth a few hours back. But this? This was new. This held hope. He rolled his head from side to side, the motion so gentle, his eyelids grew heavy. It was like an icy lullaby, and after six hours of running the maze, a relief.

The going was slow, but the wall yielded beneath his head. He forgot about running, about screaming, about kicking. He forgot about feeling foolish. Who cared? At last he was getting somewhere.

The giggle stopped all his progress. Hank felt his eyes grow wide. Certainly his mouth hung open. A giggle. A girl's giggle. He stepped back and surveyed the wall.

"Hello?" His voice sounded rough, so he coughed to clear it.

Nothing. Right. Walls didn't giggle. That didn't stop him from trying again. "Hello?"

"Is someone there?" The voice sounded light, but steady, and even better, real. Not some computer-simulated thing—and Hank knew all about those. This was a real girl.

Or, at least, Hank hoped she was. Instead of jumping back, he surged forward and cracked his head against the wall.

"Ow." His voice sank into the walls around him, and it was almost like he hadn't spoken at all.

"Are you okay?"

"I head-butted the wall."

"You can't do that," the girl said. "You've got to go slow."

"I know that."

"And use body parts that haven't hit the wall, either."

"I know that too." Or, at least, he did now.

"Does your head still work?"

What kind of question was that? Hank stared at the wall so hard, the surface blurred red.

"I mean," she said, "since you hit the wall with it."

Oh. Of course. He was an idiot. "Let me try." He eased forward, resting his head against the wall. From one side to the other, he rolled his head, the cold dulling the pain from the bruise.

His feet remained in the same spot, but the wall felt pliant under his forehead. He brought up a hand, testing the surface not with fingertips that had scratched, but with the heel of his hand. The sensation didn't register at first, but a small circle beneath his palm radiated warmth.

"Do you feel that?" he asked. "The heat?"

"I do."

"What do you think it is?"

A moment passed, a single heartbeat of hesitation. "Us?"

Was it? The reflex to jerk away nearly had him on the opposite side of the corridor. Instead, he stretched his fingers and pressed them against the wall. Warmth ran along his skin, pooled in his palm. The girl. It had to be, standing like he was, her hand against his.

"What's your—?" he began.

The claxon alarm rang. The walls faded. The floor vanished beneath his feet. The plummet stole his breath, felt endless until the jolt of hitting the ground. He found himself in the assembly yard, like he had after every twelve-hour shift, along with all the others in his class. Lines formed for the dining hall. By rote, Hank joined one.

"Hey, Hank!" someone called.

He didn't answer. Instead, he traced patterns across his palm. If he closed his eyes, he could still feel her warmth. When he opened them, Hank realized one thing:

He didn't even know her name.

## Eppie

Eppie scanned the dining facility, gaze darting, hopeful and quick. Too many times, she'd spotted someone, someone like her, someone with a secret. Her heart would speed up. She'd open her mouth to call out, raise a hand to wave, only to have that someone turn away.

Could she find the boy? If so, what then? How would that help them tomorrow, when they both went back inside the maze? She took her seat and pushed her dinner around her plate. Eat, she told herself. Build up your strength. Tonight's stew was smooth, at least. And hot. The center of the spoonful burnt her tongue, and the heat of it seared the back of her throat.

Eppie clutched her water cup, brought the rim to her lips, and drowned the heat. When she set the cup down, the sharp gaze of a matron fell on her.

"What did you do?" her friend Chara asked.

Eppie shook her head. "I didn't do anything." Except make the maze move. Except talk to a boy, who was somewhere beyond the yellow dividing line that ran the entire length of the dining facility.

But what if the cadre had seen Eppie and the boy, heard them talk? Well, what of it? Eppie folded her arms across her chest. She raised her chin and stared back at the matron.

The woman glanced away.

"Eppie ...?" Chara said.

Eppie put a finger to her lips. "Not here."

She was scraping her plate clean when the bell sounded. Normally, they'd be released into the yard for a precious hour of social interaction, but not at this point in their training, not while they were all navigating the maze. Instead, they walked the lines to their separate dormitories, were pushed through showers, and watched the lights flicker above their bunks.

"Wakeup at zero four hundred, ladies," the matron said. "That comes awfully early."

"Actually, it comes at the same time every day," Chara whispered.

Eppie giggled. The feel of it in her throat made her think of dancing with the maze. The boy. His warmth.

"There's more to the maze," she whispered to Chara.

The matron's footfalls sounded in the aisle between the two rows of beds.

"I'm not sure it's a maze at all," she added.

The footsteps grew louder, then slowed, then stopped —right beside Eppie's bunk.

"Cadet Langtry?"

"Yes, Matron?"

"If I were you, I'd conserve my energy by not speaking."

Eppie stilled her breath even as her thoughts raced. "Yes, Matron."

So they knew? They must. If the cadre couldn't use the maze to observe them, then they had planted something in their uniforms, a tracking device, perhaps. A sudden, delicious thought of flinging off her uniform filled her head. Flinging it off and running through the maze naked. Flinging it off and finding that boy. He'd keep her warm.

Now *that* would be a dance worth doing.

## Hank

Hank stood at the entry point to the maze. He was alone in his own little corridor. They all were. If he held still, he could hear the others, their breathing, an occasional shoulder slam against the wall. No one liked going in, but the sooner they did, the sooner the day would end.

Day thirteen.

When his door whooshed open, Hank took soft steps. He let his fingertips skim the wall, the gentlest of touches. He could hold a baby bird and not injure it. Still, the cold against the soles of his feet, and the idea of the girl, urged him forward, faster and faster.

Soft and fast, he chanted to himself. Soft and fast.

Could he find her? He'd thought of her—dreamed of her—all night. Was she thinking of him? Dreaming of him? Did she even want to find him?

In nearly two weeks, what they'd both discovered yesterday was the first thing that hadn't hurt. He wanted more of that, so after half an hour (by his guess), he decided to cozy up to the wall.

He veered right, simply because he was right-handed. Hank hesitated. Was that predictable? Or maybe no second-guessing? The maze probably hated that. After all, he did.

Hank froze, his palm against the wall's surface. When, exactly, had the maze started having opinions?

"But you do," he whispered. Was it sentient? Would it eat them? It hadn't bothered to in the past twelve days, so he didn't see why it should start now.

"Do you have a name?" he asked, his face close now to the bright white of the wall. "I was stupid," he added. "I didn't ask the girl what her name was. I'm worried I won't be able to find her."

He stood now, both hands against the wall, his face inches away, legs spread. "Can you help me?"

Beneath his palms, something shifted, as if a wave deep within the wall itself had rolled past.

"I'm sorry," he added, "I didn't know I could hurt you. I only thought they were trying to hurt us."

The wave surged past again, stronger this time, carrying him with it.

"Got it," he said, feet scurrying to catch up. "You want me to go that way."

Hank ran, faster than he could on his own. With that wave beneath his palm, he nearly flew. Cold air blasted him in the face. His eyes watered, and his mouth went dry. But he didn't care.

He was flying. He was going to find the girl.

## Eppie

Eppie kept her uniform on. Tempted as she was to chuck the whole thing, the air was too frigid. Plus, at the end of the shift, did she really want to end up in the assembly yard completely naked? No. No, she did not.

Today, when her fingertips met the wall, the surface gave, just a bit, beneath the pressure. Nothing too hard, nothing violent, but yet, when she pressed her whole hand—not just the palm—against the wall, she felt herself sink into it.

"Do you forgive me?" she asked. "We didn't know. They never said." And here she was, talking to the wall as if it were a real living thing. Was it? She pressed deeper into the surface and the wall swallowed her hand, up to her wrist.

"Oh!" It didn't hurt. In fact, it made her think of what it might be like to push your way into a marshmallow. During her first year at the Academy, they'd had those, complete with a campfire that threw sparks into the air, the sweet smell of burnt sugar filling her nose. Back when things had felt hopeful, the Academy a lucky break.

Eppie eased her other hand into the wall. "What went wrong? Was it always supposed to end this way?"

The surface moved under her touch, like it was melting, except it was still far too cold for that. "You are so cold," she said. "That doesn't seem right."

Could a living thing be so cold, even one from another planet or dimension, or wherever this thing was from?

She let herself fall forward, arms spread wide as if for a giant hug. If the maze didn't catch her, she'd break her nose, maybe some bones. But she closed her eyes, let gravity take her, and fell head first into the marshmallow wall.

Three inches from the floor, the maze caught her.

"Thank you," she whispered. "I knew you would."

At that moment, something rolled over her. This was less of a marshmallow and more of a thick wave of frosting. With it came a whoop and a flash of heat. Heat. Warmth.

The boy.

"Hello!" Eppie clambered to her hands and knees. She was fully inside the wall now. She slogged forward. It felt like pushing through a meadow of velvet grass with stalks that grew taller than her head.

"Hello!" she called again, louder now. "Are you there?"

"Is that you?"

*Of course it's me*, Eppie wanted to say. But she knew what he meant. "From yesterday, right?"

"It is you!" he said. "And the maze, it somehow—"

"Brought us together." Even the ice cold interior couldn't cool the blush that flashed across her face. She didn't know what this boy looked like, didn't know his name. All she knew was that he liked to head-butt his way into things, that he was loud, that he was trying to find her.

And that made him oh so interesting.

"I'm over here," she said when he didn't respond.

"Yeah, that's just it. I don't know where 'here' is."

He laughed, and the maze around her shook. Gentle waves made the velvet insides quiver and sent her this way and that.

"The maze likes that," she said. "It likes to hear you laugh."

"How do you know?"

"I'm inside it, inside the walls."

"How on earth—?"

Eppie laughed. "Probably not."

"You're right about that," he said. "But how?"

"Remember the trust falls from first year?"

"I hated those."

"Same idea."

"Will you help me?"

"I don't know where you are." Eppie held her arms out, fingers investigating the velvet that surrounded her. His heat. She should search for his heat. But all that met her fingertips was more frigid air.

"Hey." His voice was soft. "Before I forget. What's your name?"

"Eppie Langtry."

"I'm Henry, Henry Su. But everyone calls me Hank."

"Can I call you Henry?"

"Uh, I guess. Sure."

"I don't want to be like everyone else."


### Hank

He'd found her! He'd found the girl. Hank didn't even care that she wanted to call him Henry. No one ever did.

In fact, Hank liked that he could be Henry, if just for this girl.

"I'm over here," he called.

"It's like you're everywhere." She laughed, and the sound flowed through the space, seemed to fill it.

"I think it likes it when *you* laugh," he said.

"So you think it's ... something, too."

"Yeah. But I don't know what."

"I almost want to say it's not here."

"Oh, it's here."

"I mean ..." She sighed, and that too, traveled through the walls. "It's from somewhere else, or another dimension, one that was rolled up small, but now is stretched thin." She paused, then added, "That's why it's cold. That's why it hurts."

"Who did the stretching?"

This time, Eppie's exhale filled his ears. They both knew the answer to his question. Whoever did the stretching also shoved them inside every morning.

"Why did it pick us?" Hank asked, his voice quiet. "I mean, you're special." Hank knew she was. The trust fall proved that. "But I'm nobody. Average grades, average test scores, average everything."

"I don't believe that."

"I can prove it. On the outside, at least."

"Maybe it's not what's on the outside that counts."

"So what do we do?" he asked. "How do we help it?"

"I don't know. The only thing I do know is that I want to feel your hand again."

Hank swallowed, hard. For a full ten seconds, he quite possibly forgot how to breathe. "Maybe." He coughed.

"Maybe I should hold still, and you try to find me." He cleared his throat again and added, "It might be easier that way, since you're on the inside."

He let himself melt into the wall. The surface grew softer beneath him, more pliant. From somewhere deep inside the wall came a whooshing noise, a sloshing that sounded like someone pushing through knee-deep water.

"Have you ever seen a wheat field?" Eppie asked.

"Only in vids."

"This must be what it's like, walking through one, only the stalks are so soft."

A spot of heat brushed against his palms.

"Oh, I found you!" Eppie cried out before he could utter a word.

They stood like that, palm to palm. A circle of heat bloomed beneath their hands, spread into the wall itself.

"Do you feel that?" she asked.

Hank coughed again. "Yeah."

"I think it wants us closer together. You know, more points of contact."

"You okay with that?"

"Why wouldn't I be okay?" she said. "It's like dancing."

Well, he wasn't going to use that word, but yes, like dancing. They eased closer together. Was that her cheek against his lips?

"Why do you think it needs us?" he asked.

"I don't know."

"Do you think it's ... I don't know, using us? Not in a bad way. I mean, I barely know you, but I couldn't stop thinking of you last night. You know?"

"Yeah, I know."

"It feels ... right, and yet, nothing makes sense."

"Nothing about this last year makes sense. Weren't you excited to get into the Academy?"

He had been, just like his older brothers.

"I wasn't expecting it to be easy," Eppie continued. "But even the training that seemed stupid at the time had a point, and you kind of knew what that was, even if you didn't exactly."

Hank snorted. That was the Academy, all right. "Both my brothers graduated from here. Frederick never talks about the maze, and all Jon says is don't stop moving."

But they had stopped. And now?

"All that training," she said, "and then they put us in here, and it feels like ... it feels like—"

"A mistake," he finished. "Someone's made a mistake, and they don't know how to fix it."

"Then why are they sending class after class through the maze?"

"Maybe they were hoping for the right combination?"

"Maybe they were hoping for us. Look."

Shadows played against the walls, the ceiling, and even the floor of the maze. Dark figures ran, punched walls, scratched and kicked. Hank wanted to scream. *Stop! You're not helping.*

"More than one dimension, then?" Eppie asked.

"I wasn't paying attention that day in class."

"I think this goes beyond anything they teach in class."

"That's probably part of the problem."

The claxon bell blared, echoing through the maze with enough force to rupture an eardrum. Hank felt it shake the walls. The surface beneath his hands trembled, like a wild creature racked with fear and pain. Before the bottom fell out—before the walls melted and his feet slid through nothing—he lunged forward.

Forget trust falls. This was a trust dive. He grabbed Eppie around the waist the same moment she clutched his shoulders. He wasn't losing her this time.

The second before they hit bottom, Eppie said:

"Don't let go."


## Eppie

Something about the assembly yard was different, and it wasn't simply because she was clutching the boy, Henry. They held onto each other, and Eppie took in the grass beneath her, the sky above, a twilight blue with a nearly full moon. And yet, when she stared hard, she saw the maze, or the outline of it, floating above their heads.

Others saw it too. Faces turned skyward. Necks, some long and slender, others thick and sturdy, were all she could see of her classmates. Another dimension? A being? Whatever it was, things were different.

Matrons and wardens converged on the yard, corralling boys and girls, not even caring that they mixed the groups.

"Find them!" someone shouted.

"Eppie!" Chara dashed up, breathless, hair streaming from its regulation bun. "They mean you."

For the first time, Eppie's gaze met Henry's. His soulful dark eyes looked worried. "Us?" he said.

He sprang to his feet and reached for her. Eppie

grabbed on with one hand, pushing herself up with the other. Then, still clutching Henry, she ran. Their classmates parted for them, then filled the gap behind, forcing the wardens and matrons to shove, to pull out the tazons. Zaps, sizzles, and the cries of their classmates echoed behind them.

"What are they doing?" Eppie forced out between breaths.

"Something bad."

"What did we do?"

Henry glanced at her before sprinting harder. "Something bad?"

They raced past their classmates, intent on those last few steps to freedom. The protected forest around the Academy would shelter them. She knew enough, Eppie was sure, to survive for days in there, despite the lack of supplies. The two of them together? They'd make do.

At the very edge, where the scent of pine filled the air, and branches reached out as if to greet them, they slammed into a wall. Not like one from the maze. This wall was thick, electrified. It sent Eppie backward, through the air, her grip torn from Henry's.

Her hip crunched against the earth first, a sickening sound that made her think of broken bones. She rolled, hoping that would absorb the shock. She rolled and rolled, right into a pair of white, gleaming boots. She stared up into the glowing end of a tazon.

Eppie never raised her hands. Her mouth stayed closed. She held on, held her breath, and braced for what would happen next.

The jolt shot through her entire body, and then her world went black.

## Hank

Hank had ended his day surrounded by black. Now, waking, it was all he saw. He reached out a hand, waved it, blinked, and waved it again. Nothing. Either the cell was lightproof, or the tazon had blinded him.

Or both. He'd heard about the cells. They all had. The cadre sent you there when you acted out. You were meant to reconsider your choices in this space, contemplate whether the rules were really that bad, whether the wardens and the matrons truly mistreated you.

*Life choices. We all make them*, the superintendent had intoned during first-year orientation.

Yeah. What a choice. All he'd done was what? Figure out the maze? Where was the reward for that? The accolades? He pushed himself up, tucked his legs beneath him, then reached a tentative hand above his head.

A meter, maybe a meter and a half. Not enough room to stand and barely enough to turn around. He inched his fingers along the walls, the floor, and the ceiling. The surface snagged callouses on his hands, the texture rough-hewn and unmoving. He scraped a knuckle and warm blood oozed between his fingers.

His head swam, an ache spreading across his skull. A panel slid back. Light flooded the space. He squinted, trying to peer out his cell, the panel, the door—or what he thought was the door—anything to give him more information.

"The prisoner is awake," someone said.

Prisoner?

"Ah, very good." A shadow crossed the open panel. "Comfortable, Cadet Su?" a smooth voice said. "I imagine fraternizing with female cadets is a great deal more fun than this."

What? He never ... well, sure, he thought about Eppie, but they'd just met—sort of. Plus, they'd been inside the maze. All rules were off.

Weren't they?

"Hungry?" the voice asked.

In response, Hank's stomach rumbled. Stupid, stupid. It made him look weak. Of course, getting thrown into a pitch-black cell didn't make him appear all that strong, or smart, either.

"Well then," the voice said, the solicitous tone chilling Hank's thoughts. "Why don't we have a little chat?"


## Eppie

The straight-back chair was unremarkable except for one thing: Eppie couldn't move. Her bare feet were flush against the floor. The surface flashed hot, then cold. She jerked against invisible bonds, unable to break contact. Sweat bathed her forehead, trickled down her spine.

"You're making it too hard on yourself," the matron said. "Simply tell us what happened. Then you can go back to the dorm, have a nice dinner, see your friends."

A false promise. She'd been trained—they all had—in resisting interrogation. Why did this matron think such simple offers would work now? The floor flashed again, a searing heat that forced a yelp from her throat.

*That.* It was one thing to read about torture, quite another for someone to cook the soles of your feet.

"You know," the matron said. "Cadet Su told us some interesting things."

The matron was all sly words and looks, playing mostly good cop. Eppie had braced for the inevitable switch—a new matron, or a warden, even. Pretending that Henry had said something might be standard procedure. In this case, it wasn't logical.

"He told us what you did."

What she did? Or what they'd done together? Neither of which amounted to much. Or perhaps, it amounted to so much that no one could understand what had happened. Eppie pictured the maze floating above the yard. The cadre wanted to control something they couldn't comprehend. And good luck with that.

"You can't hide anything from us," the woman said. "We have it all on vid, for playback, any time we like."

Then why bother asking? Eppie clamped her mouth shut. She'd stuck with the canned response, the one the cadre themselves taught. Name. Rank. Serial Number. You open your mouth, you give them an opening. Speak and you'll eventually say something you don't mean to—or can't take back.

"So, you don't mind that Cadet Su, that Hank, betrayed you?"

Perhaps someone named Cadet Su would betray her. And Hank? Well, how could you trust a Hank? Eppie shut her eyes and pictured Henry, his dark silky hair, his warm hands against her, around her waist, palm against palm as they ran. Maybe the Academy did have vids. But clearly their knowledge didn't add up to much if they didn't know the difference between Hank and Henry.

Eppie stared straight at the matron and laughed.


## Hank

He knew the beating would come the moment laughter burst from his mouth. Cadet Langtry had betrayed him? Eppie? The few glimpses of the girl he'd had over the past two days told him how rock steady she was—much more than he was, that was for sure. How smart she was. After four years of training at the Academy, couldn't the cadre see that?

Maybe they did and figured he was the idiot in the equation. Well, that was partly true, because he had just laughed, loud and long, at their ludicrous suggestion. Another round with the tazon? Sure, why not? Tossed, bruised and battered, back into his pitch-black cell? Not surprising.

What surprised him were the questions—not the ones about Eppie, but the others. What was the maze made out of? How did they get inside the walls? (And really, only Eppie had, so why ask him?) The cadre controlled the entrance and exit, herded them through the maze day after day. Yet, they knew so little. Which made him, and Eppie, and their classmates what? Lab rats?

He pressed gentle fingers against his eyes. They were swelling shut, both of them, not that it mattered inside the cell. Still, it was so dark, he was afraid he'd forget whether his eyes were open or closed. He wondered if Eppie were doing the same, testing her own bruised eyes. He hated to think of her that way, hated that maybe it was all his fault. He pressed a hand against the wall, wishing for one intense moment that it was the maze again, that he'd detect her warmth, find her again.

"Henry?"

The soft voice made him bolt upright. He should have smacked the hell out of his forehead and given himself a second concussion. Instead, the rough stone gave way—like in the maze.

"Eppie?"

"I'm here."

"Where's here?"

"Inside the maze."

## Eppie

Eppie couldn't say when the floor beneath her bruised limbs cushioned rather than punished. Her hip stopped aching, then her ribs. She dozed, possibly, before her eyes went wide with amazement.

She was inside the maze again, but it was more than that now. Actually, when she considered it, the maze had always been more than that. It was something unto itself. And it wasn't tethered to this world any longer. It had broken free. They'd seen that in the yard. But it hadn't left. It had come back.

For her?

Yes, and not just for her.

"Let's find Henry," she told it.

And so they traveled. High above the Academy, Eppie breathed in the panic below. Hovercrafts for on-planet use, space transport, footlockers and bags scattered in the yard, and parents streaming through the halls in search of their children. Her stomach tightened. Her own parents? Had they been notified? Or was she not part of that world anymore?

The maze carried her through the long corridors of the Academy. She eavesdropped on hurried meetings, press conferences cut short. A scandal, with two cadets dead due to unauthorized experiments.

Dead?

"Please," she told the maze. "Where's Henry? Is he all right?"

So they floated lower, and lower, beneath the first floor, the basement, into the catacombs that fueled so many rumors among the cadets.

"All true?" she wondered out loud.

They passed her own cell. Her uniform, ghostly white, flat and listless, was crumpled on the floor. Perhaps the urge to lose her uniform had been right all along. She certainly didn't need it now.

A sob echoed through the dark hall and wrenched her heart, but she was powerless to console the mourner. The maze continued down the hall, down another level. Eppie held up her hand, like she had the first time she'd met Henry inside the maze.

"I'll know him," she said. "Just go slowly."

And so it did.

"There. There he is." That telltale warmth, the palm that fit against her own. Henry. "He's never been inside," she added. Not like she had. She knew the maze, and it knew her, but Henry? They hadn't gotten to that point.

"I think he'll trust you now. Will you try?"

And so the maze did.

"Eppie?"

"I'm here."

"Where's here?"

"Inside the maze."

He coughed, and his whole body shook with it. The maze trembled as if it too were in pain.

"Let go," she told Henry. "Just let go."

"How?"

"Take my hands."

Palm to palm, then laced fingers. She pulled him up, the now useless uniform empty and deflated on the floor.

"Where are we?" Henry asked.

"I'm not completely sure, but I think we're inside a baby universe," she said. "It was an experiment, here at the Academy, for years and years, and no one knew."

"Except for the cadets they ran through it."

"Exactly."

"So what is it now?"

"Now I think it's evolving." Her voice was hushed. "And I think it's evolving because of us, because we tried to find each other, because—"

"We knew there was something more."

They floated up, up, up, out of the catacombs, through the Academy, and hovered over the chaos of the yard. Then they went higher, into the stars.

"It'll need room to expand," Eppie said.

"Babies can't stay little forever."

Eppie laughed and shot forward, her form ethereal now. Henry caught her, and they twirled.

"Someday, we'll have to settle down," he said. "All three of us."

But for now they were simply a boy and a girl, with an entire universe between them.

*The Maze* was first published in *The Maze: Three Tales of the Future* by Collins Mark Books, July 2014.

## Inside Out

THE DAY LEXIA discovered the glass wasn't fogged was the day she decided to see the outside for herself. Something swirled beneath her hand whenever she tried to wipe the condensation from the window. A few bursts of light would shine through, then the clouds reformed, opaque as ever. Behind her, hot mineral baths churned up steam. The heated pool sent out waves of moist air. Sweat bloomed all over her skin until she glowed.

But beneath her fingers, the window was cool. Light shined behind the glass, the effect like winter on Earth—a glare to make you shield your eyes and glance away. Why? The question pinged in the back of her mind. Why would someone hide the outside?

Lexia wore her flimsy spa wrap, but didn't care. She'd see the outside, if not through the glass, then some other way. In the last year, she'd learned that there was always some other way. She cast her gaze about the spa. A group of women, her mother among them, sat at the far end, each encased to her shoulders in diamond-speckled mud.

A year ago, Lexia would have sat nearby, let the women pet her, buy her trinkets from the gift shop, listen to her mother's mock protests.

"Oh, but you'll spoil her," her mother had always said, followed by a secret smile that told Lexia no amount of spoiling was ever enough.

That was before her mother embarked on another marriage—her fifth; she was a professional decorative— before their fights. Now, relaxing felt like work, pampering a chore. So Lexia turned her back on the women and went in search of something more substantial.

Like a vent. All this moist air needed to go somewhere. And somewhere had to be better than here.

With all the steam, and chatter, and strains of soothing music, no one noticed when she rounded a corner. Or almost no one. An old lady, her gnarled fingers curled around an old-fashioned book, glanced up and gave her a smile, the sort that said she knew what Lexia was up to— and highly approved. Heart thumping, Lexia dipped out of sight and confronted the nearest vent. She pried her fingers beneath its rim. To her surprise, it slipped right off. For easy cleaning, she imagined. Not that Lexia had cleaned all that much in her sixteen years.

She eased inside, replacing the cover as best she could. Lexia crawled, hiked up her wrap, and crawled some more. The change in pressure clogged her ears as she moved from one air lock to the next, through invisible filters. The air cooled, took on a metallic flavor. Churning and clanking filled her head. It was like moving through a huge metal beast, and she was somewhere deep within its innards.

One dark turn led to another until she confronted an actual door. She punched in the code she'd seen Paulo use on the gift shop register. The door slid open, revealing a grate, and beyond that, the outside.

"Oh! That worked." She laughed, the soft sound bouncing around the enclosed space.

Tiny streams of sunlight lit the backs of her hands. There was only one thing to do. She flattened her palms against the hatchwork and shoved.

The sun's glare hit her full in the face. Lexia blinked. Tears burned her eyes and streamed down her cheeks. When a shadow blocked the light, Lexia squinted, ready to bolt back inside the spa.

But wait! It was a girl. Like her! Or almost. This girl was thin, with enormous eyes. No hair. Not a single strand marred the smooth surface of the girl's head. No eyebrows, either, Lexia realized. Still, this girl looked so pretty, and so nice.

"Hi," Lexia breathed. "Do you want to come in?" She'd read that the local population was transplanted from Earth. Certainly this girl understood her.

The girl backed up, pebbles scattering in her wake, and turned from the vent's opening. Lexia threw herself forward, latched onto an ankle, her own chest scraping rocks and metal.

"Please don't go! I won't hurt you!"

The ankle in her hands stilled. Lexia unfurled her fingers bit by bit, convinced the girl would bolt. Instead, the girl turned around and crept forward until they were face to face, Lexia leaning over the vent's edge, the girl just below her.

"I'm Lexia."

The girl took Lexia's hand, turned her palm skyward, and traced lines with a finger. Puzzled, Lexia shook her head. The lines continued, up and down, over her skin, like a child learning the alphabet. Oh, the *alphabet*.

"You're Amie!" Lexia exclaimed, unsure if she should feel clever or not.

The girl, Amie, nodded.

"Well," Lexia said. "Come on inside."

Together, they crawled through the vent. At the entrance to the pool area, Lexia pressed a finger against her lips. She slipped from the opening and casually strolled around the pool area, collecting items as she went —a robe, a head wrap, someone's oversized frothy drink. Back in the vent, Aimie gulped the drink, the foam coating her upper lip in strawberry red. Lexia draped Amie in terrycloth from ankle to head, a nearly perfect camouflage for a girl from the outside.

Outside. It was almost too much.

"Come on," Lexia said when Amie set down the drink. "My room has everything we need." She took Amie's hand, and together they left the spa.

No one noticed. Or almost no one. Lexia swore that same old lady stared at them. The smile was still there, only now it was tinged with worry.

———

IN THE HALLWAY, Lexia's stomach jumped each time a guard strolled by. They were all tall, all handsome, all with sharp eyes no amount of solicitude could hide. She led

Amie through the corridors, not too fast, but not so slow someone might notice a girl who didn't belong. Only when they had reached her quarters, and the door had whooshed closed behind them, did Lexia let out a breath.

"We did it!" She grinned at Amie. "And you need a bath."

Lexia filled the tub and drained it twice, and still gray scum floated to the top of the water. But at least Amie looked clean and—more importantly—now smelled like lavender and vanilla. Even better, the girl's dark eyes glowed and although she was silent, her smile filled Lexia's heart.

It was after the bath, and a tray full of chocolates, that Amie pointed at the model on Lexia's desk.

"I get to do one every month," Lexia said, her hand lighting on the structure. It was her best one yet, a scale replica of the first station on Mars. "Since it's a hobby, I can't do more than that. I always tell myself to go slow, make it last, but I can't stop myself."

Amie cocked her head, brow furrowing.

"I wanted construction, you see. I have the test scores for it, all the spatial ability. And I love geometry." Lexia shrugged. "They keep telling me I'm too pretty, that it makes more sense to be a decorative, like my mother, and her mother. It's a better career choice—a safer one."

She leaned closer, and Amie did the same, so their noses almost met over the top of the Mars structure. "Some girls even cut themselves." Lexia drew an imaginary blade along her cheekbone. Amie jumped back and shook her head, her eyes wide and scared.

"Oh, don't worry. I won't. Besides, do you see anything

sharp in here?" Lexia laughed, but it was the bitter sound she sometimes heard from her mother. She clamped her mouth shut. "Do you know how hard it is to build anything without something sharp?"

Amie's gaze went to the Mars station, then lighted on Lexia's face. Her hand moved again, first in the air, then on the table surface, like when she'd taught Lexia her name, but different.

"Oh, plans," Lexia said at last. "You're wondering if I draw plans. I can, but—"Why hadn't she considered this before? No, it wouldn't be nearly as fulfilling as building a model, but it beat waiting for her nail polish to dry or dozing through yet another facial.

She pulled up two chairs to her in-room console. She scrolled past all the social chatter, the notices for *Slam Tonight!* and the spa offering a "me" day, and dug into the educational programs. Yes! Design and Drafting, architecture, everything to teach her how to build virtual houses, cities, even stations that could be used anywhere in the galaxy, from research centers, like on Mars, to ones like they sat in now—a spa facility meant for rest and relaxation.

Lexia tore her gaze from all the potential plans and speared Amie with a look. "Did you know about this?"

Amie grinned and gave her a shrug.

"Do you need help with something, on the outside? Is that why you're here?"

Amie leaned forward and pressed the keypad. On the screen, images of makeshift dwellings appeared. Amie pointed to one and then to herself.

"You live ... there?" Lexia shook her head in disbelief.

The wooden structure was little more than a lean-to. Sure, Lexia had done her time in Adventure Girls. Once, she had even slept outside, with nothing but canvas stretched over her. But at the end of the trip, the entire group had returned to a spa facility, where every pore was sucked clean, hair and nails made to shine.

Amie tapped Lexia's wrist. The girl pointed to the screen, and then to Lexia. With her hands, she mimicked building.

"Do you want my help? Want me to show you how to make it better?"

Amie gave an emphatic nod.

"Okay." Lexia pulled her hair into a loose bun at the base of her neck. "Let's see what I can do."

———

IT TOOK A WEEK OF DESIGNING, of visualizing, not just on the screen, but in her head, and when she could, in real time. Lexia took to collecting odd bits the spa guests left lying around. Old-fashioned books, empty containers from box lunches. These she fashioned into a small village. She learned, by watching Amie move stick figures around the structures, about life on the outside.

She knew that—somewhere—her console time was being logged. Keeping up appearances meant venturing from her quarters. She'd loved school, but a girl destined to be a third-generation decorative spent most of her time experimenting with foundations rather than building them.

But leaving her room meant leaving Amie behind.

Unless ... Her fingertips lighted on Amie's bald head. Even when the look was in fashion (and it currently wasn't), it attracted too much attention.

"Want to go somewhere?" she asked, feeling sly.

Amie's eyes went wide, but her lips curled into a smile.

"I'll get you a wig," Lexia said. "And then we can really have some fun."

———

IN THE GIFT SHOP, Lexia ran her fingers through the strands of a pink wig, one with spring-green highlights. A presence shadowed her steps, tall and broad. Paulo stood behind her. Paulo, who keyed in codes on the register so sloppily, Lexia often wondered if it were on purpose.

"You going to wear that to the slam tonight?" he asked.

"I might."

"Haven't seen you at one."

"My mother's been giving me fits." Actually, she hadn't seen her mother in nearly two weeks, at least not up close, but it was a handy excuse.

"Sneak out tonight." With the suggestion, Paulo winked.

"I might," she said again. *Always keep them guessing.* This was her mother's advice when it came to men. When Paulo grinned, Lexia saw that it did, indeed, work. But it was an empty sort of victory. Why build castles in the air when she could construct real places to live? Who needed boys when she had a friend—a sister—waiting for her, one who needed her help?

———

FROM HER VANTAGE point in the hallway, Lexia could see the wide-open door of her quarters. When her mother's voice barked commands, Lexia almost ran away. One thought kept her locked in place.

Amie.

Lexia swiped the sweat from her upper lip and considered the wig, tissue-wrapped and snug in a spa bag. Another command echoed from the room and a guard stepped out. He blinked, surprise washing across his features before he schooled them into a bland expression.

"Ah, Mrs. Mortarri? I think I've found her."

He nodded at Lexia, and she had no choice but to enter her room.

"You're not in that much trouble," he whispered as she passed.

If he thought that, then he didn't know her mother.

"There you are!" Her mother whirled, hands on hips. "Where have you been?"

"Nowhere. A walk." Her voice sounded strained, shaky. She clutched the ribbon handles of the bag and willed herself not to search for Amie. *Don't move. Don't glance around. Don't breathe.*

Her mother raised an eyebrow. "Shopping?"

Lexia cringed. Of course. No one cared if she spent hours in the educational modules on her console, but the second the charge at the gift shop went through, the system must have alerted her mother.

Her mother held out a hand. Lexia pulled the wig from the bag and dropped it into her mother's waiting palm. A year ago, she could have purchased three new wigs, and her mother would have laughed—and tried them all on herself.

"Really, Lexia? You shouldn't cheapen yourself with such trash, not to wear and not to associate with."

The words felt like a blow to the throat. No, she really didn't like Paulo—at least, not in the way he wanted her to—but the boy wasn't trash. He simply had to work and wanted to dance and drink when he wasn't. And the wig that was oh, so pretty? And would look so nice on Amie? Well, that wasn't trash either.

"And what is that?" Her mother pointed at the Mars station and the replica of Amie's village she'd built around it.

"A model," Lexia said, and how the words found their way from her throat, she didn't know. "I like building them."

"I'm not sure it's the best use of your time."

"It's just a hobby." Casual, not plaintive. *Don't let her see how much it means.*

Her mother shook her head. "You're just so ... just so ... well, I simply don't know what I'm going to do with you."

In earlier times—better times—her mother might have tried to understand. She'd sit on the floor with Lexia, both of them surrounded by building blocks, and laugh when her own constructions inevitably collapsed while Lexia's remained standing.

"You must get it from your father," she'd say, "because clearly you didn't get it from me."

Soft words no longer came from her mouth. Not since last year, since her last, awful marriage. She never spoke of Lexia's father. It was as if she wished both of them would simply fade away. They no longer shared quarters. Lexia was never invited to her mother's dinner parties; not that she wanted to eat with a bunch of adults. But eating alone, in her quarters, made everything taste the same, like salt, even the desserts. Especially the desserts.

As if she had no more words for Lexia, her mother left, without a goodbye, a kiss, a hug. Lexia stared at the shut door. Oh, that she could burn a hole into it with just her eyes.

"I'm what, Mother? Just because you don't care about the things I do, doesn't mean I'm—"

A pair of thin arms wrapped around her, a soft sigh bathing her neck. Lexia spun, mouth wide open in wonder.

"Where did you—?"

Amie pointed to the bed, or rather, the platform it sat on. Lexia knelt, rapped her knuckles against the side, and listened to the hollow sound. She eased back the panel and peered inside. Beneath the bed, there was just enough room for an Amie-sized girl.

"You're smarter than I am," she said. "I don't even have your wig, and now we can't—"

Amie pressed a finger against Lexia's lips.

"I talk too much, don't I?"

Amie simply drew her to the console. There, she scrolled through the fashion channels until the display landed on turbans.

"Oh, but those are for old ladies." Lexia wrinkled her nose. "Like my mother."

Amie opened her mouth in a silent laugh. Then she pointed to Lexia's collection of nail polish.

"Oh!" Lexia jumped up, fingers tingling like they always did before a new project. "I could make it pretty." She spun around. "I could start a trend."

She tore a strip from the bottom of her bed sheet. Around Amie's fragile head it went, then Lexia sprinkled on glitter and sparkles, and dotted the material with lime green nail polish. Lexia turned her friend toward the mirror.

"Look at you! You're gorgeous."

Amie's eyes glowed, her fingertips touching the dots that matched her nails.

Lexia clapped her hands. "Let's go have some fun."

———

ONLY IN SHOWING Amie the spa did the oddities strike Lexia. Why, with the sun so brilliant, was the glass perpetually fogged? Why was everything so self-contained? At the last spa, she'd gone on excursions nearly every day, took lessons in the local language, and even visited the planet's tiny moon.

Here, there was one short day trip to an island resort owned by the spa—and nothing else. The information panel talked up the splendors of the planet, the town of

New Eden, the sustainable lifestyle of the local populace, and the fresh produce brought in daily to the spa.

Then she thought of Amie's lean-to and all the plans she somehow hoped to give the girl. She thought of the disease that had stolen her friend's voice as a baby. Why hide these things? The only thing on the other side of the glass was reality.

"Is it bad outside?" she asked Amie. They'd discovered the kitchens, now deserted after the formal dinner, and were working their way through a tub of berries and cream. Here was the food of New Eden. For once, Lexia was hungry. For once, things tasted sweet, and her fingers grabbed one berry after another, as if she'd never get enough.

Amie shook her head.

"But it isn't easy."

Amie shrugged and dipped a palm-sized strawberry into the cream.

"Why were you trying to get inside, then?"

Amie froze, mid-bite. Her gaze darted toward Lexia, a pleading look in the girl's eyes.

"For the same reason I was trying to get out? Just to see what was on the other side?"

Amie swallowed the strawberry and threw her head back in silent laughter.

————

MAYBE IT WAS the berry-stained fingerprints left in their wake. Maybe it was the pilfered sparkling quenchers from the walk-in refrigerator. Or maybe the guards had simply tracked their every move since they had left Lexia's quarters.

No matter. The first guard caught Lexia unaware, thick fingers around her wrist and upper arm. Amie, though quicker, fared no better. She kicked, tried to scratch, her mouth open in a silent scream.

Lexia screamed for her. Her cries brought officers and old, respected guests, and too many witnesses.

"They're hurting her," someone said, voice ringing with indignation.

An old woman hobbled into the center of the gathering. "Let the child go," she said to the guards.

The man holding Lexia released his grip on her. She rubbed his sweat from her skin and tried to wipe away the ache.

"Now the other," the old woman added.

The guards released Amie as if her skin burned them. The second her feet touched ground, she scampered off. No one chased after her, and Lexia let out a sigh that shook her whole body. She turned to thank the old woman, but froze. Yes! It was the same woman, the one in the spa, with the book and the secret smile. And now that smile bloomed again on the old woman's face. Before Lexia could say a word, a barking voice cut through the silence.

"Lexia! What have you done!"

Her mother parted the crowd with her voice and a hand—the same hand that, seconds later, cracked against Lexia's cheek.

Lexia stumbled into the guard behind her. His hands gripped her waist for longer than strictly necessary. She didn't care. Her cheek stung, her eyes watered, her heart squeezed tight in her chest.

"Mind that she is still a child," the old woman said.

"Mind your own business," her mother snapped.

"You could say I am. Is she not my granddaughter?"

Her mother paled. Lexia felt all the air leave her lungs. She focused on the old woman, her soft face, and eyes that looked both sad and kind.

"Technically, no," her mother said. "She is not."

"But as long as you're married to my son ..."

Her mother's mouth went grim. The old woman hobbled over to Lexia.

"We have not met, my dear, and I suspect we won't again. A piece of advice from an old woman, then?"

Numb, Lexia nodded.

"Don't let yourself get trapped. I did. So did your mother. That's not a sufficient reason to end up trapped yourself."

The woman kissed the bruise forming on Lexia's cheek and turned down the hall. The crowd, the guards, silent and staring, parted for her. No one spoke. At last, her mother gave a frustrated sigh, collared Lexia, and dragged her through the corridors by the spa wrap.

———

WHEN HER MOTHER engaged the override lock, Lexia pressed her hands against the smooth door. Her first impulse was to pound, to kick—just like a child. Instead, she leaned her forehead against the cool surface and shut her eyes. In her mind, Amie ran through the hallways, into the pool area, and crawled through the vent to freedom.

She wanted to believe the pictures in her head. An icy fist in the pit of her stomach told her it was better not to.

What had gone wrong? Why was *she* always wrong? She never sneaked out to slams, like the other girls, never even flirted with the spa workers. All she wanted was a friend. Lexia had never known that that hole inside her existed until Amie had filled the space. Now, nothing but an ache remained, that hole larger and darker than ever.

Her gaze lighted on the bed, or rather, what it sat on, its hollow platform. She crawled, wrists aching, and eased back the panel. Could she fit? She wasn't as small as Amie. Inside the space smelled old, like layer upon layer of dust and memories. Lexia eased her feet to the farthest corner, settled her hipbone near the center, and at last pressed her cheek against the floor. The bruise throbbed, but it was a handy reminder. If she was truly going to do what she planned to, she'd need that.

Lexia packed, weighing each item for its potential worth and inevitable weight. In went all the plans and designs she'd made with Amie. Although it was frivolous, she added the lime-green nail polish. From her bed, Lexia tugged the smallest blanket and rolled it tight. Then she curled into the hollow space again, belongings at her feet, blanket beneath her sore cheek.

It took a very long time to fall asleep.

———

IN THE MORNING, her mother's shrieks woke her.

"Where is she?"

"Sorry, Mrs. Mortarri, but there's no record at all of anyone entering or leaving her quarters."

"But she's not here."

Lexia held her breath. Would they search for her? Could anyone detect the panel, in place, but slightly off-kilter? Would anyone use an infrared detector, or for that matter, common sense?

"I suppose someone could have hacked the system," a guard ventured.

"That boy from the gift shop. What's his name?" Her mother snapped her fingers. "I don't know, but find him. Find her!"

Poor Paulo, Lexia thought. He didn't deserve this. The stomp of boots filled the room before footfalls echoed down the corridor. She squirmed, peered through the small sliver where the front panel didn't quite meet the corner of the headboard. Her mother wore a spa wrap and a wash of tears across her face. The urge to shove the panel out of the way nearly overwhelmed Lexia. In her mind, she saw the scene play out. She'd burst from her hiding spot. *Here I am*, she would say. Her mother would embrace her, kiss the bruise on her cheek, and cry even after Lexia forgave her.

She braced her feet against the wall, ready to push back the panel, but froze when the intercom buzzed.

"Mrs. Mortarri, will you be keeping your massage appointment this morning?"

"Excuse me?" her mother said. "My what?"

"Massage appointment. Under the circumstances, we can reschedule."

Lexia's chest grew tight. Her head buzzed, and the sound of it was so loud, she was afraid she'd miss her mother's next words.

"Yes, of course I'll keep my appointment," her mother said. "It's been a stressful morning."

And now Lexia couldn't breathe.

Her mother turned, the spa wrap fluttering across Lexia's field of vision before vanishing completely.

Where had her mother gone? Her real mother, not the one who had so recently swept from the room, intent on keeping a massage appointment. Where had that woman run to? Because certainly she'd gone somewhere and left Lexia behind, alone with an imposter.

She slipped from under the bed and replaced its panel, then she tore a few more strips from the bottom of her sheet. These she used to tie the blanket to her pack.

At the door, she hesitated, rocking on the balls of her feet. Would it open for her? She had shed the spa wrap, and what she guessed was the tracking device that went with it. She wore old clothes, from Earth—out of fashion, of course—but they were nondescript and sturdy. Lexia shut her eyes, inhaled a deep breath, and placed her hand on the console.

The door opened.

She grinned—couldn't help it. In a way, it made sense. Why engage an override lock on an empty room?

In the corridor, a guard passed her, the same one who had gripped her wrists and left his sweat all over her. The man stared as though he didn't recognize her. Maybe he didn't. Maybe that was part of the problem with these spas. Everyone was either a guest or a worker—no one was an actual person.

In the pool area, she rushed past the mud baths, the mineral pools, running her fingers along the fogged glass without leaving any streaks. Lexia paused near the cabana where her mother booked all her massages.

The flaps were closed.

She clamped a hand over her mouth and wished she could cry silently like Amie did. Then, she turned toward the vent.

She crawled through the structure's innards, spilled onto the pebbles outside, and scrambled to her feet. The spa sat behind her, a white blob, its own self-contained bubble in a brilliant green reality. Hills stretched for miles. Lexia ran, haphazardly at first, then with purpose toward the largest tree on the first hill.

On one of the branches, something white flapped in the wind. When she was ten feet away, she recognized it.

A strip from Amie's turban.

Lexia stood beneath the branch and peered at the path ahead of her. Another glimmer of white, there, in the distance? She slid down the hill, never losing sight of the bit of white. When she reached the second tree, she tugged the strip from the branch and tied it around her wrist. Then she ran toward the next hint of white in the distance, leaving the world of fogged glass behind.

*Inside Out* was first published in *The Maze: Three Tales of the Future* by Collins Mark Books, July 2014.

## About the Author

CHARITY TAHMASEB has slung corn on the cob for Green Giant and jumped out of airplanes (but not at the same time). She spent twelve years as a Girl Scout and six in the Army; that she wore a green uniform for both may not be a coincidence. These days, she writes fiction (long and short) and works as a technical writer for a software company in St. Paul.

Her short speculative fiction has appeared in *Flash Fiction Online*, *Deep Magic*, and *Cicada*.

# Also by Charity Tahmaseb